HomeWars

DOROTHY REYNOLDS MILLER

A JEAN KARL BOOK
ATHENEUM BOOKS FOR YOUNG READERS

Books by Dorothy Reynolds Miller

The Clearing: A Mystery
Home Wars

Atheneum Books for Young Readers
An imprint of Simon & Schuster Children's Publishing Division
1230 Avenue of the Americas
New York, New York 10020

Book design by Nina Barnett
The text of this book is set in 13-point Weiss.

First Edition
Printed in the United States of America
10 9 8 7 6 5 4 3 2 1
Library of Congress Cataloging-in-Publication Data
Miller, Dorothy Reynolds, date.
Home wars / Dorothy Reynolds Miller.
p. cm.
"A Jean Karl book."
Summary: Twelve-year-old Halley sees her family torn apart when her father gives her
teenage half brothers antique flintlocks, which begins an escalating argument between her
parents about the dangers of guns.
ISBN 0-689-81411-9
[1. Firearms—Fiction. 2. Gun control—Fiction. 3. Stepfamilies—Fiction. 4. Family prob-
lems—Fiction.] I. Title.
PZ7.M61265Ho 1997
[Fic]—dc20
96-38584

Dedicated with love to my daughters

1

It's summer, and we're at the Dragon. Kirk and I are throwing damaged ears of corn and rotten tomatoes over a stand. The object is to get them over the roof of the stand and into a fifty-five-gallon drum that's sitting on the other side where we can't see it.

I'm throwing tomatoes this time. I've already won with corn, so I tell Kirk, "I'll do tomatoes, because maybe corn's easier." I get five tries, and then he gets five.

I haven't known Kirk for very long, only since the beginning of summer when his grandfather bought the warehouse and moved in. At first I thought he wouldn't want to hang around with me, because boys usually just like hanging around with boys. But after I talked to him, and he figured out I wasn't going to ask him about makeup or to play Barbies or anything, he started being my friend.

I'm winning, but it's no fun beating Kirk. What I really want to do is beat my brothers, Mike and Johnny. That's what I'm thinking when I look up and see them coming down the lane—with guns! "C'mon," I say to Kirk, and we race to meet them. They're going to Mom's stand.

When they get there she takes one look at them and exclaims, "Guns!" Mike and Johnny nod happily. She gives them a hugely negative look. "They're not real . . . !" Her voice quavers. ". . . are they?"

They do some more happy nodding.

"Where did you get them?"

"Dad," they both answer, and they're still grinning.

"Tim got you guns!" Mom exclaims. "I can't believe this!"

Now they're beginning to get it. The grins start to fade, and they look around, like anywhere else is a better place to be. All of their excitement and pride is melting away—melting, melting, gone.

There are four guns, and they are very long. It seems funny to me that Mike and Johnny just walked in with them and didn't know what to expect. I would have. But then I usually think they don't know anything.

Mom looks at the guns like they are poisonous snakes. "Put them there," she says, gesturing to the corner beside the trash cans.

"Aw, Mom," Mike begins.

She cuts off further protest with a snapped, "Get your father." Her lips are pressed tightly together, and I can practically see steam shooting from her ears. Mike's thinking of saying something else, and he hesitates, but Johnny has already taken off up the lane. Mom begins warming up. "Guns! The imbecile!" Mike takes off and catches up with Johnny.

I can't decide what to do. Dad's going to get a terrific chewing out, and I'd like to stop it, but I probably can't. "Maybe they're not real," I try.

She glances at them with loathing. "Oh, they're real, Halley!" It's like she could say a lot more, but wants to save it for Dad.

Kirk is perched on the old bench nearby, but he's looking out across the pond. My white Persian cat, Bentley, is winding along a table, carefully stepping over old silverware. I run my hand down her back, and purrs boil out of her.

The Dragon is just one long street with several little side streets. It stretches down along a curve in the creek, and from above it looks like it's being held in the creek's arm.

The streets aren't paved, they're just oiled dirt. Dad knows about places like this because he's a history professor. He told me the Dragon was once an old fort, but a long time after it was a fort, people called "bootleggers" moved in, and then the main part of the town left and moved up the hill.

There are buildings called "stands" all along the main street, and a few of them on the side street that goes up to the parking lot. They were once log houses. Most of them are closed in the back and are open in the front.

Each one has a different kind of business, like cloth and yarn, greeting cards, clay and ceramics. One makes handmade shoes for people who have clubfeet. The blacksmith shoes the fox hunter's horses. The Isaac Walton has fishing lures, and the bakery has beautiful wedding cakes. The shop up from it has every kind of sour thing—pickles, sauerkraut, and borscht. Mom's stand is filled with antiques—ceramics, jewelry, and books.

Between the backs of the stands and the parking lot

there are old, twisted trees. The whole Dragon is so old, it's historic, and sometimes people come from the university to work on the archaeological dig. Other people come there to sit and paint, but the only person who paints the Dragon so you feel like you're there is Squirrely Akers, the man who hauls fruit.

There are open spaces that are like yards between the stands, and on evenings and weekends people come there and back their trucks in. They park them and sell things from the backs of them—mostly vegetables and fruits.

Kirk and I are across from Mom's stand. We're hanging over the hitching rail in front of the blacksmith's, and it's like we're waiting for a battle to begin. Bentley's winding through my legs, and I pick her up and balance her on my shoulder.

Dad doesn't come. After a while Kirk actually says, "Let's go back and throw some more corn and tomatoes." It's unusual for him to suggest anything. Usually I do the suggesting.

"Okay," I agree, even though I don't really want to. It's a hot summer day, and it's almost noon. Dad'll come down for lunch, and I want to watch for him.

Kirk and I are both twelve. Mike and Johnny are thirteen and fourteen. They don't mess with Kirk much. He can't even play baseball as well as I can, and he's also so quiet no one hardly notices him. Most of the time he's like a shadow.

Kirk actually beats me seven times with corn. I've beaten him four times with corn and twice with tomatoes. The whole back of Squirrely Akers's stand is red with smashed tomatoes. I say to Kirk, "It looks like blood. If we told someone there was a gruesome murder here, they'd believe it." Kirk shrugs and turns away.

Kirk's grandfather, Edgar Demitros, owns the biggest building in the Dragon. No one knows anything about Edgar. When anyone asks him where he came from, he just acts like he can't hear the question.

His warehouse is full of furniture, some of it antique but most of it just sort of old, not really antique, the everyday, ordinary kind. The warehouse has always been full of furniture for sale, but when Edgar bought it, he brought several more truckloads.

Dad and Mike and Johnny are coming, and I can feel my stomach begin to tighten. Before I even get over to Mom's stand I can hear her. By the time I'm actually there, Dad's exclaiming, "Gwen, they're antiques. What do you take me for, an idiot!"

"Yes," Mom says, "that's exactly what I take you for! Giving guns to children, it's outrageous! What are they to do with them, shoot bunnies or go to war?"

"We'll shoot targets," Dad says. "Boys who are thirteen and fourteen are plenty old enough for guns. I got my first gun when I was nine. Dad taught me to shoot. It was a special time."

"I won't have it," Mom says. "They're dangerous. Boys don't need weapons. Look at those Sower kids, shooting all the time."

Dad's looking at her like she's someone he doesn't know. "I thought you'd appreciate these because of the workmanship. They're perfect. One's a Dickert, one's a Beck. I had been thinking of getting them twenty-twos, but these! They're magnificent! They belonged to an old man who collected antique guns. They're original Pennsylvania long rifles. He didn't have time to restore them, so they went cheap. We're going to work on them—"

"No!" Mom shouts. People all around are watching. "They blow up in kids' faces! Kids get to shooting songbirds. They shoot at everything that moves just to be shooting, and soon they accidentally shoot themselves or someone else. If you start them on antiques, pretty soon they'll want more modern ones. After all, they're all well made. Then you'll all have gun collections. I won't tolerate it. You should have asked me first."

Dad looks uncomfortable, and he's beginning to look hot. His eyes go from Mom to the guns leaning against the corner behind the trash cans. One person he doesn't look at is me. I'm the youngest, and a girl. He'd never buy me a gun. I'm thinking, actually, that I could shoot one and probably hit something, although they do look large.

Mike and Johnny are looking anywhere but at Mom or Dad. Dad says to Mom, "I don't need to hear this, and you don't need to get excited. The boys will be responsible." He lowers his voice. "We don't need to make a spectacle of ourselves, either. Everyone's listening. I'll take them home."

Mom doesn't care who hears. She's still at top volume. "They're not going to have them!"

"I'll put them in the garage," Dad says. Then he gathers them up and angrily stalks away.

One thing about Kirk, I don't have to explain. He doesn't ask or say any of the things he could say that I don't want to hear. When I turn around and leave, he just comes along.

Up behind the Dragon there are pine trees, and beyond them are fields. It's not very far to walk from up where we live on the edge of town. The Dragon is open all spring, summer, and fall, and sometimes people go there to sing and preach from the backs of trucks. There's always something to watch or do.

In the evening before it gets dark, the pines stand out like huge, mysterious, black silhouettes against the blazing sunset. After twilight, the lights come on, and the whole place looks like a dream, a dream that is filled with the sounds of voices and engines, the smell of exhaust fumes, fruit, dust, and pine.

The Dragon always seems like a warm, good-living place. When Mom's stand is open, we're always there. We never go anywhere else much, except to church.

We're going down the street, and Bentley already knows where we're going. She just reads my mind and then starts out for Kirk's grandfather's warehouse. Whenever I go anywhere, she never likes to follow. She's already halfway up the wooden steps to the warehouse's porch.

It's a huge, sagging building with just one story, and it's dark and cavelike. There are only a few small, cobweb-covered windows way high up. There's furniture everywhere, huge pieces stacked on top of other huge pieces, all of them so heavy they'd crush you if they fell. Between the stacks of furniture are little aisles, which make the place seem like a maze.

Kirk's grandfather, Edgar, is there, directing men who are unloading a truck, telling them where to put each piece, scooting around to see that they do it right. Edgar is a frightful-looking person. He's deformed, with short stubs instead of arms. At the ends of the stubs are large, normal-looking hands. It looks like his hands are stuck onto very wide shoulders.

He doesn't have legs, just small extensions where his legs should be, and at the end of them he has little knobs instead of feet. On his little, knob feet he wears leather booties.

To go anywhere he rides on a platform that's like a skateboard, except it's wider, and the wheels swivel and have rubber tires. He scoots over the warehouse's wooden floor very fast on his platform, using two poles to propel himself.

The poles have hooks on one end and rubber knobs on the other. When he wants to reach for something or do something, he flips the poles around very fast and operates the hooks, which have levers that make them clamp and unclamp.

He does everything with his hooked poles: buttons his shirt, zips his jacket, opens doors. When they first moved in, we watched him put up a clothesline and then hang wash on it.

Everyone wonders where he came from. Whenever I

ask Kirk about where he lived before, he just acts like Edgar, suddenly deaf. Edgar's waving and pointing with his poles, directing the men who are unloading his truck. It seems like the poles are a part of him. If something needs fixing, he uses a hammer or screwdriver with his hooks. Mom and Dad say he's an adaptive miracle.

Although he doesn't have any legs, his body, neck, and head are huge and powerful. His eyes bulge, and when he looks at someone he looks ferocious and frightful. I pity Kirk because he has to live with him.

We're standing watching men carry in furniture, and I confide to Kirk, "I was afraid of Edgar when you first moved here."

Kirk doesn't look at me or react. People who don't know him might think he's stupid, because he's always so quiet, but when there's something he wants to talk about, it's clear he can think.

After the truck is unloaded and has driven off, Edgar goes back in and hops up onto the swivel chair behind his huge rolltop desk.

Edgar has a van equipped with rods instead of a steering wheel. He makes it go and stop and turn with the rods. He and Kirk live in the back of the warehouse in a little part that's walled off from the rest. They each have a cot and they cook on a hot plate. Mom calls it primitive. I think it's like camping. It's like the cabin we rented at the state park. But I still pity Kirk.

Inside the dark warehouse in the summer, sometimes it's cooler than outside because the fans are going, and a huge box elder tree spreads its branches protectively out over the warehouse. "Let's each hide ten things and time each other to see who can find them all first," I suggest.

"It can't be in drawers or cabinets," Kirk says. "Edgar doesn't want us opening things." We're walking down one aisle when I suddenly see a picture that I've never seen before. The minute I see it I have to stop and just stand and stare. Kirk has been walking on ahead of me, but he comes back and stands beside me, following my gaze as I look at it.

It's so beautiful I can't even talk for a few seconds, but then I just say, "Oh!" It's a picture of the ocean. Just water. There's no land, no rocky shore with crashing waves, no lighthouses, no sand dunes, no people. Just endless waves of water with sky above it. Kirk looks at the picture and then at me and back to the picture. "You like it?"

"Yes, oh yes!"

"It just came in." I don't say anything, so he goes on. "It was in our old house." Slowly I turn from the picture to him.

"In your house? It's yours?" He nods. "Is it for sale?"

"I don't know." He's just looking at me.

I'm so excited. "Let's go. I'm going to ask Edgar if it's for sale."

Kirk looks alarmed. "Oh, I don't think that's a good idea. He just got the truck unloaded. He won't want us to bother him."

I can't take my eyes off the picture. I'm almost afraid

to walk close for fear that it'll have some fault, and I won't be able to think of it as perfect anymore. But I can't stay away forever, so I slowly walk to it. It's very large. The frame is carved, dark wood, and the picture is covered with glass. Kirk's with me. "It's just water," he says. I can tell he doesn't think it's beautiful.

"Don't you like it? It's the most beautiful picture I've ever seen." He turns his head to one side and then the other, looking at it as though, if he keeps looking, he might begin to see it as I do.

"It's" —he searches for the word— "restless."

"Yes!" I exclaim reverently. "It's like the whole picture is moving, and you can look at it and feel the water, feel the waves. I could look at it all the time and never get tired of it."

"Edgar won't have a price on it yet," Kirk says. "We'll have to wait until he does."

Kirk's afraid of Edgar, that's what I think. It's just the two of them. No mother or father or brothers or sisters. I don't think it would be nice to live with Edgar, but I'd never say it to Kirk.

2

Mom calls me to go home with her because she doesn't like me hanging around the Dragon when she isn't there. We're walking back along the creek with Bentley leading. If we go up the road and walk through the town, I have to carry Bentley or she'll trot down the center of the street and be run over.

While we're walking I'm telling Mom, "There's this picture in Edgar's warehouse! Can I have it, please? It's so, so perfect!" I don't get an answer. She looks mad. She's still mad at Dad.

I'm thinking it'll be a good thing to get her mind onto the picture. "I could hang it in my room, Mom. Can I buy it? I have money in the bank."

"Picture?" she asks. "The walls in your room can't take much, Halley. What kind of picture?"

"The ocean. Just water. I want it. I have to have it."

She sighs, a huge sigh. "I don't know about anything. If Tim doesn't get real about those guns, you may not even have walls. You may not even have a room. I won't be bullied by anyone, especially him. It's ridiculous."

I quickly change the subject. "Do you know why Kirk doesn't have a mother or father?"

She doesn't want to talk, but she says, "No. People

say Edgar has been here or there. Someone said he knows a lot about honey production. Someone else said he knows about dancing, of all things. He seems to have been to Greece. And England. And Ireland. It's funny—he drops little bits of information about places, here and there, everywhere. But no one can really place him anywhere.

"Tim even asked Uncle Canute if he could find out about Edgar, but he couldn't. I wonder if Edgar doesn't just make things up, spread little false hints around for fun to fool people. I wouldn't put it past him.

"Their name's Demitros, and that's Greek. One of the men at the garage said Edgar knows a lot about getting around in New York City. But then one of his drivers said he thought they came from Upstate New York. I wonder why they came here to Pennsylvania." She adds thoughtfully, "Whatever, that Kirk seems like a nice kid."

"I want to find out about them."

"Lots of luck," she says.

As soon as we get to the house we see the guns. The garage doors are open, and the guns are in front leaning against the wall. I can practically feel her anger. "Tim!" Her tone means war. Mike and Johnny come out the kitchen door.

"Dad left. He had to go to the library."

Mom's eyes narrow. "Yeah, right!"

Then Johnny says, "I was out in the yard throwing the ball up and catching it, and Mrs. Sower came out and started singing, real loud, some dumb tune over and over."

"I heard her," Mike says. "That was the tune to *The Brady Bunch.*"

"Ignore her," Mom says. "She's nuts."

Mrs. Sower is a neighbor who doesn't like us, but we can't figure out why. She's always swearing at us and calling us names. Mom thinks it's because Mrs. Sower's sister wanted to go with Dad before Mom and Dad were married.

"Your dad has to get rid of those things!" Mom gestures to the guns. "I'm not going to put up with them! They can't be here!"

"Why?" Johnny asks. "I like them. We like them. Dad says we're going to learn to shoot."

"Don't either of you go near that garage," Mom says. "I mean it. They won't even stay here till Tim gets home if I see either of you touch them."

Mike and Johnny go out onto the patio. They're looking stubborn. I know if I go out with them when they look like that, they'll just give me some kind of hassle, but there's nothing to do in the house. Besides, its shady out there. I pick Bentley up and go out.

Mike's on the swing. Johnny's on the chaise. Good deal, I get the hammock. Bentley loves the hammock.

"Our real mother would let us have them," Mike's saying. "Gwen's a jerk." Mike and Johnny are Dad's sons by his first wife. Whenever they get upset with Mom they call her Gwen. And they say, just to themselves or to me, never to Mom or Dad, that their real mother, Boots, was better. She'd do all this good stuff for them. She'd be just great.

I don't like Boots. And I don't like the idea of them having another mother, even though neither of them has seen her for years, and I've never seen her.

They have her picture, though. I know that, but Mom doesn't. It's underneath their microscope in the microscope box. If they ever knew I looked at it, they'd be furious. When I looked at it, I made sure they weren't around.

From the hammock, swinging high with Bentley, I say, "Your real mother's a jerk."

Johnny just looks out across the yard to the Sowers' house, but Mike gives my hammock a tremendous shove, and I have to use both hands to keep from falling on my head. I can't keep hold of Bentley, and she flies out of my arms.

I give a loud scream, and Mom calls out from the laundry, "What's going on out there?" None of us answer.

When Dad comes home, as soon as he walks in the door, Mom attacks. "Well, what are you going to do about them?"

"What?" he asks. He has forgotten.

"The guns," she snaps.

He gives a silent, oh, like now I remember. "Nothing, tonight. I have to mow the lawn. Tomorrow I'll start cleaning them. You don't need to worr—"

"No!" Mom interrupts angrily. "Why can't you respect my feelings! Why are you trying to run something over me! The guns can't stay here. The boys can't shoot them. You know how I feel. Why aren't my feelings important? I'll not have them here. I'll throw them in the creek!"

"You're overreacting," Dad says. "And who's running something over whom? Don't my feelings count? Those aren't just ordinary guns, they're flintlocks! They are fascinating, beautiful artifacts from the past. I was lucky to get them. They're exquisitely made, and they were a tremendous bargain. If you destroy them, I'll never forgive you. My feelings have to count, too."

"Your feelings do count," Mom says, "but when you bring something into our lives that could kill us, that could destroy us, then your feelings are going to have to take a hike in the face of common sense. I won't have them here. Read my lips, they will not be here."

Dad says, "Well, if you don't give me any more credit than that, if you think I'm a worthless idiot, a numbskull—if you think I'm such a nincompoop that you have to tell me what to do, maybe I shouldn't be here." And he stomps out and slams the door.

Mom's eyes light on us and she snaps, "Get your showers and go to bed. Don't talk to me."

Upstairs I say to the boys, "You shouldn't act like you care about those guns. If you act like you don't like them, Dad'll just get tired of them and sell them, but if you mess with them, Mom and Dad'll get a divorce."

"That's stupid," Mike says. "I want to learn to shoot. Eddie and Gary Sower each have their own thirty-thirty rifles. Mom—Gwen's just being an id— she's just, like Dad said, being unreasonable."

"She'll get calm," Johnny says. "We aren't going to

shoot anything." Bentley's winding over my shoulder and down my face.

"Except Bentley," Mike says as he points a finger at her and makes a *pow!* sound.

I glare at him. "You shoot Bentley, and I'll fix you. You'll wish you never saw me!"

"I wish I never saw you already." Mike grins.

"I wish I never saw you. You should be with your mother."

Mike narrows his eyes and glares at me. "I know we should. I don't care if Dad does get divorced from Gwen. I hope he does."

Johnny looks at him like he's saying a million swear words. I'm thinking how much I'd like to hit him if he didn't hit back so hard.

3

Dad doesn't come home that night until after we've been in bed for a long time. Mom thinks we're asleep, but we're not. When he comes home there's just slamming doors. They don't talk.

The next morning we're up and getting ready for church. "Aren't you going?" Mom asks him.

"No." He sounds stiff and mad.

Mike and Johnny try to get out of going, too. "We'll stay home with you, Dad."

But he says, "No, you won't. Go with your mother."

"Aw, Dad," they say, but it doesn't work.

When we get home from church we look in the garage for the guns, and they're gone. Dad's sitting, reading the paper. Mom starts dinner. No one talks to anyone.

It's like that for several days. Even Mike and Johnny are actually quieter. When we argue we do it so no one can hear. The only things Mom and Dad say to each other are things like, from Dad, "This isn't my home. I can't have anything I want here."

Or from Mom, "If I have to put up with something dangerous and frightening, I can't call this my home."

That's how they have conversations, not really talking to each other, just talking about what they'd say if they were talking to each other.

I spend a lot of time with Kirk. We're picking wild raspberries at the edge of a field, and he points to a bunch of brambles up where the field meets the woods. "Look at them!" he says.

I'm telling him all the stuff, like that Mike and Johnny don't care if Mom and Dad get a divorce, because then maybe Dad might go back to their real mother, and that would stink, because I'd have the divorced family instead of them. "It isn't fair," I tell Kirk. "And it's horrible!"

When I talk to Kirk he sometimes says things that don't have anything to do with what I'm talking about. Like, he says, "Wish I had brothers and sisters."

"You're just wishing for trouble."

The branches between the field and the woods are weighed down with berries. We're picking them like crazy, and our buckets are almost full. I'm sitting licking berry juice off my hand when suddenly there's a loud booming sound. At the sound, Kirk jumps up. It's a shot. He looks horrified. I'm thinking he looks like a bullet has hit him, only I just can't see it.

There's another one, and he jumps again. I hunch down and call to him, "Stay down!" His eyes are wide as he sinks down beside me.

"Where'd it come from?" I ask. We are both looking around, but we don't see anyone.

"Maybe from up there." Kirk points. "Up in the woods." We're scrunched behind some brush. I don't know why he looks so nervous.

"No one can see us here," I tell him.

We're there for a long while, and we're about to get up, when there's another one. It has a booming sound, much louder than the first two. "We gotta get out of here!" Kirk exclaims in a loud whisper. He looks scared.

"Oh, it's probably just someone doing target practice," I say to him. "Maybe even Dad. Maybe he didn't get rid of the guns, and he's up there shooting them. Anyway, it's way up. I think in the field beyond the woods."

Kirk seems a little calmer, but then there's a fourth shot, and he jumps again. I'm getting used to his reaction. "What if it isn't someone shooting targets?" he asks. His eyes are very big. I just look at him.

"You mean, like it could be criminals or something?" He nods. "And they're shooting someone and would shoot us if they saw us, because they'd think we were witnesses and could identify them?" He nods again. Actually, my description of the dangerous people who might be up there seems to calm him. He's still scrunched down, but he has a handful of berries and he's filing them into his mouth.

"My grandfather used to bring me up here to get berries," I whisper to him.

"Edgar makes coffee cake and puts them in. It's so good."

We haven't heard any shots for a while. Kirk gestures

toward the woods. "Maybe we can get up now and go."

"What if there's some guy who has just killed some-one, and he's coming down through the woods real quiet right now? If we stand up, he could see us. He could kill us right now, or if he has to think about it, he could follow us home and find out where we live. Then he could climb into a window and kill us later." Kirk just looks at me. "There could be two guys and they have a hostage, and that's what they're doing, shooting him or her."

Kirk is thinking, but then he says, "Nah," and stands up. Just then there are two more shots, and he quickly sinks back down. After a minute he says, "I could go see." Now it's my turn to just look at him.

He carefully braces his bucket full of berries against the dirt bank, and then, without saying anything, he starts slowly crawling. He's creeping up, low and slith-ery, over the bank. When he gets to the woods he slowly pushes past the little bushes and disappears.

I'm thinking, this is really a bad idea, but he keeps going and right before he disappears from my view completely I shove my bucket into the bank and start slithering after him.

It takes a long while for us to go a short distance because we're going so slowly and carefully, and we're looking around all the time. When he gets to a big tree, he eases up very slowly and then peeks around. I pick another big tree and do the same.

There's nothing, and I don't hear anything. His tree's huge, and I dash to it. "Right up there's where the shots were coming from," he whispers, pointing. "It has to be more than one person, they were so close together." He's just about to move when suddenly there's another shot, and we both shrink against the trunk. "They're way up."

"I wonder who it is?"

"I'm going to run up," he says.

I'm just about to say, "Are you crazy? Just hearing a shot makes you jump out of your skin," when he takes off. He's running, zigzagging around trees and bushes. It seems like he's running forever. He's way up, so far he looks small before he stops behind another big tree.

My heart's pounding. What if there really are bad guys? We could be two dead bodies. I wonder if Mike and Johnny would be sorry they treated me so mean. Or if Mom and Dad would get close again and cry together about me if they were staring at my dead body. I take off and dash through the woods until I'm beside him.

By the time I get up to him I'm desperately in need of air. I can't gasp because it'll make too much noise, so I have my mouth open and I'm fanning air into it with my hands.

"Listen," Kirk says, "voices."

I listen closely, and then I know. "It's Dad and the boys! I knew it!" Kirk starts to step out from behind the tree, but I grab his shirt and hiss as I pull him back, "No! I don't want them to know we're here!" He looks puzzled.

"You know why. Mom and Dad are mad at each other

because of the guns. I'm not supposed to know about this. Neither is Mom. We can't let them see us."

Kirk's looking up to the top of the ridge. We're both still breathing hard. Over our breaths we can hear them, but just barely. Dad's calling, "Clasp it harder, bring it up and tight in." Then there's the loud crack of a shot, and all through the woods the smell of smoke.

"Let's go up where we can watch," Kirk says. I nod, and he drops down and starts to slither up over a little bump, keeping behind several big trees. When he gets to a huge rock he stops behind it and carefully peeks around.

Another shot, and there's Mike's voice yelling, "Way off."

Then I can hear Dad. Something like, "Barrel hot." I drop down and creep up beside Kirk. When I get to the big rock I go to the other side and peek around it.

The field's high and it drops off to the whole valley below. The only thing higher, out in the distance, is a place called Dinky's Bluff. They're shooting at bales of straw with paper targets nailed to them.

Suddenly I want to be a part of it. There's something about the way they stand, the way they move. Like they're doing something important. Their motions are almost flowing. And then there are the things they have, new things I've never seen before. A horn from which Johnny is shaking something into the side of the gun. A bag with a long strap that's like a shoulder purse, except it looks old. There's the smell of smoke from the guns. Above them in the sky the crows are circling and scolding.

Mike's standing with the muzzle of the longest gun in his hand, the butt—with its intricate carving and its brass patch box—is resting on the ground. He's tearing fabric with his teeth. Each of his motions is so purposeful, so confident. He doesn't look the same. I duck my head back behind the rock and whisper to Kirk, "Wish I could do that." Kirk doesn't answer.

"That's the Dickert," Dad's telling him. "Small bore, long, octagonal barrel, flintlock, daisy finial, typical of Lancaster rifles. This was used in the Revolution." Crack! Fire shoots out the muzzle, and a stronger smell of smoke slowly spreads through the air.

Dad turns to Johnny. "This is a Lehigh County–Allentown rifle. See the wooden patch box and how slim and graceful it is with its double-arc curve." He's holding the gun, caressing the stock reverently. "Rifle making required the longest of all the apprenticeships. You could be a blacksmith in three years, or a wheelwright in one and a half, but to make these—it took artistry of the highest order. You had to master the art of working in metal and with wood, brass, and often silver. It had to be bored just right, and when it was done you had to know how to shoot it in order to evaluate it.

"If it was made well, it would feed a man and his family. It would protect him from enemies, and it would get him extra money for the things he and his family needed. It would even start his cooking fire. See, if you don't have matches, but you have a flintlock, you just hold a bit of lint here, snap the flint, and sparks fly. Voilà, instant fire." He hands the rifle to Johnny, who takes it carefully and handles it with a reverent look.

Johnny brings the long, slender gun up and fires. Then Dad says reluctantly, "We'd better hang this up for the day."

"Oh, do we have to!" from Mike.

"'Fraid so," Dad says. He's even talking different, like he's in an Old West movie. They start packing up, and it looks funny when they put a lot of little stuff in the shoulder purse. Except that Dad pats it and says to Mike, "We'll get some soft leather and make each of you a 'possible bag.'"

Kirk and I are perfectly still as we watch and listen. Then it occurs to me—I wiggle over to him at the other side of the rock and whisper, "What if they come past here when they leave? They'll see us."

We both look around. I see a large tree and slink back to it. Kirk starts to wiggle back to me, but just when he's away from the rock we hear them coming. He flattens himself, like he's trying to become a part of the ground.

I grab a quick glance. Dad and Mike are coming closer to us, but they're looking in the other direction. Kirk's so close to the ground that it's like he's dirt and leaves. They pass down through the woods without seeing us.

We wait until they're out of the woods and way down the field where we can't hear them, then we get up and start in the same direction, dashing from tree to tree. "We'll have to wait until they're down around the creek before we come out of the woods," Kirk says in a loud whisper.

"Yeah. Wonder where they're going. The guns weren't in the garage."

"Toward the Dragon," Kirk says. We follow, keeping way back.

At the edge of the Dragon I peep out around the end of Akers's stand and see them heading for the end door of the warehouse. "Your place!" I exclaim. "Were the guns in there before?"

"I don't know," Kirk says.

I can believe him. He doesn't ever lie.

4

After the boys and Dad are gone we go down to the
Dragon and casually walk into the warehouse like we're
just bored and looking for something to do. Edgar
scoots by. He never says anything to anyone unless it's
something about his business. We're looking for the
guns, but we have to wait until he's back at his desk
before we can search seriously.

As soon as he propels himself onto his chair and starts
looking through his books, we go down the aisles, carefully not going straight in case he's watching us and
notices where we're going.

They're stacked in the far corner, just inside the end
door. Suddenly we hear Edgar scooting in our direction
again, so we quickly dash up one aisle and stand looking in a mirror, like that was what we had been doing.
Edgar's glance at us, reflected in the mirror as he passes,
is grumpy. As usual I pity Kirk because he has to live
with him.

After he passes we wander along, going in the direction of my picture. When we get to it I whisper to Kirk,
"I'm going to ask him. I want to know how much it
costs."

"He'll never sell it."

"Never sell it! Why's it in here? Isn't everything in here for sale?"

"Uh, yeah, no," Kirk says hesitantly.

"Is he going to hang it in your place?"

"No. I guess he'd sell it if someone had a lot of money. He said we have to sell all of our things because we don't have a house here." He looks around at the furniture that's sitting on either side of us. "That was in his bedroom where we lived before. And that rocker was in the living room. He says he wants a lot of money for them, more than they're worth, because he likes them. If he likes something, he charges more for it than it's worth, because he doesn't really want to sell it."

I'm in front of the picture, and with Kirk's words I'm becoming more and more disappointed. "It's so wonderful," I tell him. "I want it. I need it." Kirk's looking at it like he still can't see why I like it. "I'm going to ask him, anyway. It won't hurt to ask. And then if it's too much, I'll just have to save until I get enough, whatever it is. Maybe I can work for Mom and make money." Whenever I mention actually talking to Edgar, Kirk looks nervous.

I get up and start toward the front with Kirk behind me. At Edgar's desk I stand and wait for him to look up. He doesn't act like he knows we're there. I'm thinking, if we were adults, he'd already be asking if he could help us.

"The picture," I begin, "the ocean one." He's still not looking at me. "Back there. I want to buy it. How much does it cost?"

His eyes bulge in his huge face, and when he looks at me I automatically take a step back. Even though he has no arms or legs he still seems large and powerful. "Don't know what you're talking about." His voice is deep and gruff, growly sounding, and he means, go away.

I wait for Kirk to tell him, but beside me Kirk is quiet. So I say, "Kirk said it was in your house. It's a picture of the ocean, just wa—"

"Three hundred dollars." The words boom out of him like a threat.

Outside I exclaim to Kirk, "Three hundred dollars! It might as well be a million. Mom'd never let me spend three hundred dollars for a picture. If I ever got three hundred dollars, I'd have to put it in the bank for my education or something."

Kirk nods like he's sharing my disappointment.

Mom's at her stand. "Don't tell her about the guns," I say to Kirk. "Remember, she can't know. She'd have even more fits, and then they'd get a divorce for sure."

"I won't," he promises. "I don't like guns."

"Why?"

He just shrugs.

"I want to learn to shoot. Bet I could hit more things than Mike or Johnny."

He just looks at me.

When Mom sees us she says, "Put Bentley's harness on and take her out. She probably has to go." Bentley's in her cage at the back of the stand. She has to stay there on Tuesdays because Akers's delivery man comes with a dog that goes insane whenever it sees her.

"Watch out for that ugly mutt when you're with her," Mom says as we leave. "And as soon as you get back she has to be brushed."

Bentley has to be brushed every day or she'll get a hair ball. She's snow white, with long, luxurious fur. I take her down to her favorite sandpile, and then bring her back up and start on her fur. She's so calm and gentle I can pose her in any position and she stays put.

To Mom I say, "The picture in Edgar's that I love costs three hundred dollars."

"A mere!" she exclaims.

"If I make the money, can I buy it?"

To my surprise she doesn't just say no. "What did you say it's a picture of?"

"The ocean. Water."

"Just water?"

"Yes, waves, water."

"Oh."

At home before dinner Mike and Johnny and I are out on the patio. Mike has the swing, and Johnny has the chaise. I get the hammock. Looking at the ceiling I just casually say, "Bet I could shoot really straight."

Johnny's eyes dart to Mike. Mike responds with a "Don't say anything" look.

"Bet I could find some guns to shoot."

"So" —Mike narrows his eyes upon me— "your twerpy little friend found them and blabbed where they were."

"No, he didn't!" I exclaim in disgust. "He didn't know where they were. I'm just an excellent detective."

Both of them look agitated, but they're trying not to show it. They're so obvious.

"So, if you know, then go tell," Mike challenges. "We don't care. Mom's the one who cares."

"I'm not a tattler," I respond. "You know that. If I were a tattler, you'd be in so much trouble all the time, you couldn't breathe."

"Yeah, we know," Johnny says. "You're not a tattler. It's just that Dad and Mom—"

Mike interrupts. "Who cares!"

5

The next day we're alone. Dad's at a history professor's conference in Chicago, and Mom's at the Dragon. I'm listening to TV when I overhear Johnny saying to Mike in a shocked tone, "We can't. Dad would have a fit."

They're in the kitchen. My radar's up immediately. They're speaking so I can't hear, even though I mentally shut out the TV and concentrate hard to catch the slightest sound.

"Ssshhhssh!" Mike says. I lower the TV volume.

They're whispering super quietly. Then they start microwaving lunch. There's a lot more whispering, but I can't hear anything with the microwave fan going. And yet it's like I'm almost getting a mental picture. I just bet—I walk in and say, "You'd better not. I'll tell if you do."

"What?" Mike says.

"You're going down to the Dragon to get the guns and shoot them, alone."

Johnny looks impressed. "How'd you know?"

"I have sonar homed in on your brains."

Mike's glaring at me. "She probably does. She has to have someone else's brain to home in on since she doesn't have one of her own." He gives me a dagger look. "Whatever we do, it's none of your business. You're not going."

"If Dad were here, he wouldn't let you go alone."

"We know how," Johnny says.

"Dad showed us everything," Mike declares.

"If you do, I'll tell."

"Go ahead," Mike says. "Then they'll get a divorce and it'll be your fault."

They grab sandwiches and slam out the door. "I mean it," I call after them. "If you do it, I'll tell."

"Go ahead," both of them hurl back.

I pick up Bentley and bury my face in her fur. She's purring at top volume. What would happen to her if Mom and Dad got divorced? She needs a home. Her nose is absolutely flat, and she is what is called "over-bred." She needs all kinds of special stuff; so much, she actually costs a lot. I have to keep things together, for her and for me. We both need a home.

I sling her over my shoulder, unplug the toaster, and head out the door. Mom says we have to unplug the toaster no matter what because toasters cause more fires than anything else, practically. Mike and Johnny never unplug the toaster. They go out all the time and just leave it plugged in.

I can see them down along the creek far ahead of me, but I stay far behind so if they look back, they won't actually see me. By the time I'm at the entrance to the Dragon they're going down around the end of the warehouse where no one will see them.

Kirk's fishing. I get to him fast and whisper, "Mike and Johnny are going shooting alone. Come on."

He looks up at me with big, almost frightened eyes.

"Come on. We'll stay back. They can't see us."

He looks pale. I'm thinking, he doesn't like guns any more than Mom. We see them far up ahead.

"Where's your dad?" he asks.

"Chicago."

"He wouldn't allow them, would he?"

"Of course not. They're just doing it because they're jerks. I told them I'd tell, and I might. If I do, they'll get in so much trouble! But then Mom and Dad'll probably have a big fight and get divorced."

Kirk looks beyond shocked.

"Mike and Johnny don't care, because Mom isn't their real mom. If she were their real mom, they wouldn't be such jerks."

Kirk's surprised. "I didn't know they weren't your real brothers."

"Well, my dad's their dad, but he was married to their mother first. Her name's Boots, and she abandoned them."

Kirk looks confused. "Are your parents really your parents?"

"Yeah. I'll tell you something, but you have to promise never to tell." Kirk nods.

"Mike and Johnny have Boots's, their real mother's, picture. Mom doesn't know it, and neither does Dad. It's in the bottom of their microscope box. Don't ever tell. They'd have a fit if anyone knew. They don't think I know, but I do. They look at it and say a prayer for her every night. She's beautiful, but she's rotten. That's what Mom thinks."

We're behind an old barn and we're waiting for them

to go into the woods before we cross the open field. After they disappear into the woods I whisper to Kirk, "Come on."

Kirk's staring at something up near the woods. "What's that?" He squints, concentrating. "Oh, Bentley."

I haven't been thinking about Bentley. "Where?"

"There. Over by that old shed."

As we cross the field I tell him, "Bent never gets lost. I trained her to always stay with me."

Kirk looks surprised. "I didn't think you could train a cat."

"You can't. Not like a dog. But I got a jar of chicken baby food and made it into little balls. Then, when she was hungry I dropped a chicken ball every so often and she had to follow me to eat. Now she thinks she has to go everywhere with me, even when I don't have chicken. But she never follows close. She's just, like, on the same planet with me. You can't get a cat to follow you and slobber on your heel like a dog."

We're halfway through the woods when we hear the first shot. We make our way quietly and stealthily to the big stone, then sink down to watch.

They're acting like when Dad was there, tearing patches with their teeth, shaking in powder, then ramming the patch-wrapped ball down the guns' long muzzles, all the movements so purposeful and assured. I'm fascinated and I'm watching them intently until I hear a groan from Kirk. His foot's in nettle, and he's grimacing.

I motion for him to wiggle further over, but when I move a big bug jumps on my arm. As soon as I flick it off something crawls over my leg. I almost scream until I look back and see that it's only Bentley's tail brushing me as she goes by.

I give her a shove. Big mistake. Instead of going back down through the woods, which is what I want her to do, she strolls right out in the open toward Mike and Johnny.

Kirk points and rolls his eyes.

Desperately, I begin to meow.

Bentley just flicks her tail like, yeah, I like you, too, we're good buddies, and keeps on going. I try several more meows, but we have to quickly duck back behind the stone when the boys hear me and turn around.

"Oh, it's Bentley," Johnny says. "She followed us, dumb cat. Why's she meowing so much?"

Any minute she's going to turn around and mosey back to us, and then they'll follow her and see us.

But she doesn't. She's digging in their possible bag. Mike moves it and gives her a shove. "Get!"

They stop noticing her and go back to talking about shooting. They have all four of the guns. Two are leaning against a hay bale off to the side, and they have the other two.

They're shooting at cans. Mike misses completely. Johnny shoots and one of the cans moves, but it isn't knocked off the bale.

I meow loudly and then duck behind the rock, but I hear Mike say, "There's another cat in the woods."

Now they'll walk over and see us. I'm braced, waiting for them to look over the rock and right down at me.

But then I hear Johnny say, "Maybe that was Bentley and it was just an echo."

"No," Mike says, "that wasn't Bentley. There's another one. I hope it doesn't chase old Bent in front of me when I shoot. This Beck could blow a hole through her as big as a thirty-thirty."

The Beck is Dad's favorite. He has a picture of one tacked up in his office, and he told Johnny the whole history of the man who made them. Mike raises it, grips it tight against his shoulder, and fires. Bentley's way off to the side, and she isn't even impressed by the tremendous sound.

Johnny shoots next, and she comes and winds around the bale where their equipment is. It's like she actually likes something about the guns, the smell of the powder or the smoke or something. She's rubbing the cleaning rag. Then she suddenly sees a bird. Her whole body tenses as she focuses on it.

Johnny's watching her. "Think she'll get it?"

"Nah," Mike says, "she's no hunter. We're the hunters."

"She doesn't need a gun." Johnny laughs.

They each pick up the other two guns, load, and then fire, and they each miss their targets completely with the bullets snaking off to the side through the grass.

Bentley, who's watching the bird fly away, hears and sees the sudden movement of the bullet in the grass, and she dashes over to it.

Johnny calls to her, "Get away, Bentley." He's loading the smoothbore.

"Go, Bentley," Mike says with a laugh. "Shoo. We'll shoot you."

Johnny looks at him.

"Run down there and shoo her away," Mike says.

Johnny dashes down, scoops her up, and brings her close to the stone where Kirk and I are hidden. His voice is right on the other side. "Go get that cat in the woods, Bent." Then he runs back, picks up the smoothbore, and shoots.

There's a spray of shot in the grass, and Bentley is immediately after it, pouncing all over the place, her tail twitching in excitement. She's sure it's a whole colony of mice darting around, and she's certain she's going to catch at least one of them.

Kirk whispers to me, "You have to tell them you're here and get her. They might shoot her."

I'm shocked. "They wouldn't shoot her. They're rotten, but not that rotten."

Mike has just loaded the Dickert, and he hands it to Johnny. "This one's the truest. The Lehigh shoots left."

"I can't shoot with Bentley there," Johnny says.

"Oh, just plug her," Mike says.

Johnny brings the gun up to his shoulder, aims it in her direction, and says, "Pow, pow, Bentley. Got that? You're dead now, fall over."

Mike raises the Lehigh. "I'll get her tail." A shot roars out, and the grass parts close behind her.

I'm screaming and running toward them. Behind me Kirk is yelling, "Halley, no!"

I leap on Mike and begin pounding and kicking him furiously. He has the Lehigh in his hand, and I've surprised him, so I get in a lot of punches and kicks. "You tried to kill Bentley, you creep, you dirty, rotten creep! I'll kill you."

Johnny grabs Mike's gun, and Mike gets my arms. I'm still kicking and screaming furiously.

Kirk's standing with both of his hands on his face.

Johnny grabs me with his arms tight around my waist and squeezes my breath out, but I'm still kicking and trying to scream. Finally he manages to throw me on the ground. Bentley sits near me, ever so delicately licking her front paw and carefully cleaning between each of her toes.

Johnny leans down and shouts at me, "He wasn't really aiming at Bentley!"

But Mike, furious, declares, "Yes, I was! The next time you come snooping around with that old 'Bent out of Shape Halley Cat' I will plug her."

I scoop Bentley into my arms and press her soft, warm fur against me. She rubs her whiskers along my face and purrs out her love and contentment in long, bubbling whispers.

With Bentley in my arms and Kirk following, I just run. Down through the woods and halfway through the field. I'm shaking with horror and rage.

At last, when I slow to a walk, Kirk says, "They were only pretending." He looks pale and he sounds like he's trying to convince himself.

"No they weren't! You saw how close that bullet came. Mike even said the Lehigh didn't shoot true.

They would have shot her! If I hadn't saved her, they would have." I'm staying in front of Kirk so he won't see the tears that are burning two paths down my cheeks.

He doesn't say anything for a while. But then I glance back at him and he says, "Edgar shot our donkey. I didn't want him to, but he did it, anyway."

I can't really think of anything because I'm so angry, but I'm glad Kirk's talking about something else and not noticing me. "You had a donkey? Why? Why would he shoot it?"

"It was Edgar's. It used to pull him in the cart when he went out to the field. He didn't have the ATV when we . . . where we lived."

"But why did he shoot it?"

"Because we had to leave. He didn't want to give it to someone who might abuse it. Its name was Jasper, and it was . . . nice."

"And he just shot it!"

"Yeah."

"Why'd he have to go out to a field? Were you farmers or something?"

"No . . ."

It's always the same when I ask Kirk anything about his past. He starts to say something, and then it's like he has to think about it and take out a lot of what he was going to say. "So, what was he?"

"He had beehives, and Jasper pulled him out to them in the cart."

"You mean like for honey?"

"Yeah. He smoked them."

"He smoked bees? Like cigarettes?"

Kirk starts to laugh. Then he repeats, "Like cigarettes," and he has to laugh harder. Soon he's bending
double. When he stops laughing enough that he can
talk, he gets out, "He puffed smoke into the hives so
the bees would be calm while he got the honey." He's
still laughing.

What I really feel like doing is crying furiously, but
Kirk talking about something completely different is
making me a little calmer.

"Bees get quiet and confused when they're smoked,
and then they don't sting. But he still made me wear a
suit that made me look like a spaceman when I went
with him. He never wore a suit. He always said bees
wouldn't sting him, and he didn't care if they did."

"Did they sting him?"

"No."

"If I were a bee, I wouldn't sting Edgar. I know he's
your grandfather, but . . . it's his look. I don't mean
about being . . . deformed."

"I know."

"Why didn't you take the donkey and hide it?" I grab
a glance at him. He's looking at me like I have suggested
he should just float in the air fifty feet off the ground or
rob a bank or something.

"I . . ." He hesitates, then goes on. "I didn't know he
was going to shoot him until he got the gun."

"How did Edgar shoot a gun?" I'm trying to imagine.

"The same way he does everything else."

"With his sticks?"

"Yeah."

"Would you have hidden the donkey if you had known?" I sneak another glance, because I think I know the answer. Kirk would never challenge Edgar. I don't think I would, either. I'd be afraid he'd grab me with his sticks and cut me up or something.

Kirk doesn't answer me right away, and I think he isn't going to, but then he says, "I wouldn't have known where to hide him, and someone would just have found him. Anyway . . . I wouldn't want to do something to make Edgar mad."

"Is he mean to you?"

"No, but he gets mad easy."

"He doesn't beat you?"

Kirk looks at me like I'm being ridiculous. "No, he gets mad because of his arthritis. His spine hurts."

"Where did you live before you came here?"

"I can't tell."

"Why?"

"Because . . . Edgar says not."

"I get it. You're criminals." Kirk gives me a sharp look, and I say quickly, "That's okay. I won't tell."

"No, we're not criminals." He looks shocked.

"Why can't you tell, then?"

"I don't know."

I look at him. "Yeah, sure."

"I mean it, I don't know."

"Don't you have a father or mother?"

He shakes his head.

"You have to."

"I don't . . . it was . . . a long time ago. I just know about where we used to live. I don't remember before that."

"I got it, you're stolen!"

He looks at me with wide, gray eyes. "No."

"You could be. It happens all the time. It's always on TV. Your parents were busy and they looked away, and then he stole you or something."

Kirk's slowly shaking his head. "Edgar wouldn't do that."

We're walking along, and I'm imagining this really beautiful family that's heartbroken because they've lost their beloved child. They miss him and don't know where he is.

But Kirk starts talking and ruins it. "Edgar wouldn't want me if he didn't have to take care of me. Besides, I remember stuff."

I just look at him. He looks very sad. I really like the nice family, and I don't want to get rid of them. "What stuff?" We're above the Dragon. I gently drop Bentley over the fence and start climbing.

"I had a mother," Kirk says.

I perch on top of the fence and wait for more. But he's climbing, too, and he doesn't say anything else. Sometimes Kirk's like Edgar. He says one thing, and that's it.

Up the street Mom's talking, probably to a customer. I finish climbing over the fence and then slide down to the bank on the other side.

Kirk drops down beside me. "Are you gonna tell

about them having the guns?" he asks. I scoop Bentley up and hug her so tight, she struggles and claws to get free.

"Yeah, I guess. But there's something I have to do first. Up at our house. See ya in a little while."

I leave running, with Bentley scurrying to keep up. I have to think about Mike and Johnny, and Bentley, and all of us. I don't have time to think about Kirk.

6

No one's in the house. Mom's at the Dragon, and Mike and Johnny are taking their good old time coming back. They're guessing they could be in trouble. I race up the stairs and back the hall, passing the doorway to my room, going on, into their room, and over to Mike's bed.

There, I bend down, reach underneath, and pull out their microscope box. Lifting the microscope out, I get their mother's picture. All the while, I'm listening. If I hear someone my plan is to push the picture back down, slap the microscope in on top of it, and shove the box back under the bed at the speed of light before they get to the stairs. Then I'll just be coming out of the bathroom, like that's why I'm there.

Bentley's not making it any easier. She's winding around me and rubbing herself over the picture, getting in the way, like she's saying, what have we here? I give her a shove. "Scram, Bent. I'm doing this for you. They think they can just kill you, but they'll find out."

I'm working very quickly, taking the picture out of the frame. It's big. I'll have to carry it under my shirt and keep my arms crossed over my stomach to hold it. Their mother, Boots, is beautiful, but I don't care.

I grab a piece of tablet paper from Mike's desk and quickly write, *If you shoot Bentley, I'll burn this.* Then I put the note where the picture was and quickly reassemble the frame. When they get the picture out to look at it, the only thing that'll be there will be my note.

I almost shudder when I think of how they'll react. But I don't care. If they're going to shoot Bentley, they're going to lose their mother's picture forever, and it's the only picture they have of her. I don't like her, anyway. I don't even know her, but I don't like her. Mainly because she didn't take them with her. She went to Las Vegas to deal blackjack in a casino. My life would be so much simpler if she had taken them along.

I pick up Boots's picture and stuff it under my shirt, holding her face next to my stomach. Then I dash out the door, but I have to go back because Bentley isn't with me. She's in the kitchen, rubbing her food bowl. "You can't have anything now," I tell her, "and you have to come with me. You'll have to walk. I'm saving your life. I'm going to endure torture because of you." I reach down and, holding the hidden picture to my stomach with one arm, lovingly caress her soft fur. Then I run out the door to the Dragon, with her racing to get in front of me.

When I get to the Dragon, Kirk's bouncing a ball off the warehouse roof. Mike and Johnny are shooting baskets at Harmony's fruit stand, which means they're trying to throw a basketball through his sign. It's much harder than shooting a plain, ordinary basket.

"Come on," I call to Kirk without stopping. He catches

up with me as I race up the wooden steps of the warehouse.

"Better put Bentley down," he says. "Edgar doesn't like cats."

I'm thinking, Edgar doesn't like anything. Edgar's at the entrance, sitting at his desk. He gives us a bulge-eyed stare as we walk past. I half expect him to growl, "Play outside," like he usually does, but he's concentrating on his account books and doesn't say anything.

I lead the way back through the maze of furniture. At my ocean picture I kneel down and motion to Kirk to kneel down beside me. "See this? It's Mike and Johnny's real mother."

Kirk looks at it, surprised, and then says, "She's a pretty lady."

I make a face at him. "She's not so special. Mom doesn't like her, and neither do I. Remember I told you they look at it every night? I'm going to keep it here so they don't kill Bentley. I left them a note."

Kirk looks wide-eyed. "They're going to be really mad."

"Yeah, too bad. I'm going to put tacks on my floor at night so if they try to come in while I'm sleeping, they'll step on them and scream. They won't get me, and I don't care, anyway, even if they do. I'm doing this for Bentley, to keep them from shooting her. They went too far."

Kirk nods like he understands, but he looks doubtful.

"Help me put it behind the ocean picture. No one'll buy it because it costs so much. And they'll never know where to look. Anyway, I'm saving the three hundred dollars, and I'll soon own it."

Kirk braces himself and leans the big picture forward, holding it steady, all the while looking in the direction of Edgar. I carefully feed Boots's picture down between the picture and the backing.

Then we lean the picture back, and I sit and look at it. It's so beautiful. Even in the darkened warehouse, just looking at it gives me such a feeling of joy.

Bentley's rubbing her ears on my leg. I reach down, pick her up, and wrap my arms around her.

"She sure does purr loud," Kirk whispers. "She must have just walked right past Edgar. I guess he didn't notice."

We're sitting there and he says, "Wonder if there are any pictures of my mother."

"Is she dead?"

Kirk answers softly, "I think so."

"And your dad, too?"

He nods.

"How'd they die?"

He looks up to the ceiling and then away down an aisle, anywhere but at me. "Maybe there was an explosion."

"What! Do you remember one?"

"Maybe. Kind of. Sort of."

"What kind of explosion?"

"I don't know."

"Ask Edgar. You should know."

"I already did, but he won't say."

I'm feeling really frustrated. "Well, I want to know!" Kirk is gravely shaking his head.

We leave the warehouse and go to Harmony's fruit stand to ask for a box of rotten oranges. Carrying them between us, we head for the back of the old shed, passing Mike on the way. I don't see Johnny. He has probably gone up to the house to watch TV. As Mike goes by I say to him, "You're going to be sorry."

He makes a face at me. "I don't care if you tattled. You'll be sorrier than anyone if you did." I just glare at him.

We throw the oranges into a bucket for a while, and then we're just playing catch with them. They're not as messy as rotten tomatoes. Kirk pokes eyes and a nose and a mouth into one that is half covered with fuzzy mold. With the fuzz and the eyes and mouth it looks like a funny head.

"Mom said that mold gives you cancer," I tell him. He looks worried, and quickly rubs his hands on his shorts. I'm thinking, that's what happens when a kid doesn't have a mother to tell him the stuff he needs to know.

"What kind of cancer?" he asks.

"I don't know. Maybe of the hands."

We're tired of throwing fruit, so we go down to the pond, to the place where Kirk keeps his fishing stuff. He retrieves his can of night crawlers, threads one onto his hook, and throws it in.

The pond is made by a dam. Ducks are swimming all around it, and two of them have fluffy little yellow ducklings. Out in the open the sun is melting hot, but beside the dam, where we're sitting, all around us are weeping willows, their branches swaying softly and drooping to the ground like strands of long, green lace.

"I hear thunder," Kirk says. "It's going to storm. When it storms, our roof leaks. I think that big tree outside my window could fall and crush us when it storms, but Edgar says it won't. I don't know how he knows."

I look back up to the huge old tree standing with its gigantic branches stretched out over the warehouse. "Trees just all of a sudden are hit by lightning," I tell him. "Then they crack and come down. You could be killed. Does the warehouse have a basement you could go down into?"

Kirk shakes his head. "Edgar says that lightning would hit the locust trees up by the fence first before it would hit us. He says locust trees attract lightning."

"You mean they're like lightning magnets?"

"Yeah, I guess."

"Edgar tells you a lot of stuff."

"We don't have TV."

"I like where you live, with the cots and hot plate and stuff. It's more interesting than a regular house. Where we live it's boring. And I like it out here with the willows and ducks. It's like living in a state park all the time."

Kirk's looking in the water. "Yesterday two men came around and asked a lot of questions about Edgar. Harry, you know, the truck driver, told Edgar they had Irish accents. Edgar looked mad, and he said if anybody came around again asking about him, to tell them he sold out and went to Brazil."

"Brazil! Why? You're not moving to Brazil, are you?"

Kirk just shrugs and continues staring into the water. After a couple of seconds he says, "There are snappers in there."

I'm pulling my toes back. "Snappers?"

"Yeah, big, ugly turtles. You better keep your feet away from there." I pull my feet further back.

"Edgar says he's going to start catching them soon, and then we're going to eat them."

"You're going to eat turtles?"

"Yeah."

"Yeccchh! Did you ever eat them before?"

"No."

I'm looking at the peaceful water out where his bob- ber is floating, barely moving. "How do you know they're there, the snappers? Did you see them?"

"Edgar says so." He looks around at me. It's like he's thinking of something, but is trying to decide whether to tell me.

"At night, sometimes, it's real quiet, and we're in bed listening to the radio. But when Edgar shuts it off, and we aren't asleep and are just listening to the outside sounds, mostly crickets, or like owls and stuff, you can hear the water coming into the pond from the creek. Except sometimes, all of a sudden, you hear a duck just squawk and squawk.

"First there's this fast quacking, and then a kind of gurgling and squawking? One time I asked Edgar what it was, and he said a snapper had just gotten hungry again and had surfaced and grabbed a duck and was pulling it down and eating it."

I'm just looking at him. Now the pond is ruined. Just

like that. Before, it was beautiful and peaceful. The ducks were happy and safe, hatching eggs with beautiful little ducklings, eating bugs and being happier and freer than any other living thing, practically. But now in my mind they are swimming above, like, crocodiles, what would be crocodiles to them, and just waiting to be chosen for drowning and death. It's horrible.

"I hope Edgar catches every last one of them and you eat them all. Except that, do you realize when you're eating them you'll be really eating duck, too?"

Kirk nods and grins. "Like if chickens eat bugs and you eat chicken, you're really eating bugs?"

I act like I'm gagging. "Don't say that, please! You'll make me hate chicken!"

Bentley loves night crawlers. She's lying on her back with the can in her paws, trying to figure out how to get them. Kirk has the can covered with a rag and a rubber band so she can't get them.

I pick up a stick and I'm stirring the water, jabbing it in every now and then, hoping I'll jab a snapper. "Mike and Johnny are rotten," I say to Kirk, "but I still don't like telling. I'm no tattler." Kirk pulls up his line and checks it.

"I mean, why can't they just go and live with Boots? She and Dad were divorced before she had Johnny, and then he married Mom. But Mike and Johnny lived with Boots until they were five and six. I didn't even hardly know them until I was four. But then she decided to go to Las Vegas and she just came one day and left them with Dad.

"I sort of remember when they came, even though I

was only four. No one thinks I remember when they didn't live with us, but I do. I can remember a long time before them. Can you believe I thought they were fun at first and I liked them?"

Kirk says, "I had brothers and sisters. Edgar doesn't think I remember. But I do—some stuff really well. I'll always remember when he found this place. He was reading, and then he suddenly said, 'Business for Sale,' real loud. He said it sounded perfect for us."

"How old were you when you didn't have a family anymore?"

"I don't know."

"Squirrely Akers told Mom that Edgar has been to Greece. Were you ever in Greece?"

"I don't remember."

"People are always saying things about Edgar, but it's like they're all blind and he's an elephant," I say, and Kirk looks around, puzzled. "You know, like the poem where a lot of blind men are trying to figure out what an elephant looks like just by feeling it, except that they can't because it feels different to each one of them. To the one who's holding its tail, it feels like a rope, and another one grabs its ear, so he thinks elephants are shaped like fans, and the one who's feeling its trunk thinks it's like a snake. That's what it's like with people trying to figure out about Edgar." Kirk looks at me and grins.

I'm getting to know him better and better. He never looks mean or mad like Edgar, but when he doesn't want to talk, he means it. From that I can tell he's Edgar's real grandson.

"Mike remembers Boots really well, but he never talks

to anyone about her except Johnny. Johnny doesn't
remember her as much, so he asks Mike stuff and then
Mike tells him. When she dropped them off she told
them she'd come back for them soon, but she didn't.
She never even called.

"They found that picture of her down at Uncle
Canute's one Christmas. It was in a box in his garage,
and they just took it. When Dad found it, he threw it
in the trash. Then they got it out and hid it in their
microscope box. Want to know how I know they get it
out every night?"

Kirk nods.

"After I found it I put it in the box a different way, and
then looked the next day. It was put back different. So
I put it in another way, and it was different again.

"Then I put my tape recorder under their beds and
recorded Johnny saying, 'You can hold it tonight, and I
get to tomorrow.' When they say their prayers and
they're supposed to be praying for their parents, they're
really praying for her, not Mom." Kirk keeps his eyes
on the bobber most of the time, but he glances away
from it and toward me every now and then. "They
think if they don't pray for her she'll die."

"Do you think she'll ever come back?" he asks.

"No. If I knew what her address was in Las Vegas, I'd
write to her and tell her to come and get them. But if I
did that, and Mom and Dad found out, they'd be really
mad. They'd probably send *me* to live with her. At least
Dad would. Mom might, even. I wonder how I could
find out her address? What I don't understand is why
they can't pray for Mom."

"Don't they ever?"

"Yeah, but it's just like, 'And Mom 'n' Dad,' like they're one person. For her, they say, 'Please bless Mommy and take care of her.' Isn't that sickening? They still call her 'Mommy.' I haven't called Mom 'Mommy' since I was about six."

"I called my mother 'Mum,'" Kirk says. He looks like he has just discovered something he didn't know before. "Edgar wouldn't want me to say anything about it."

7

I'm putting off telling Mom about Mike and Johnny having the guns. But then I get the idea of telling it like it's someone else and not really them, so she can just sort of deal with it but not really know. Kirk has given up fishing and he's dirt biking up and down the bank. I'm lying on the grass nearby, thinking, with Bentley wrapped around my neck. She's so soft and innocent. I'm thinking, I just can't let them kill her, so I get up and start for Mom's stand.

When I get there I have to wait until there's a break with no customers. And even when the customers are finally gone I have to stand around thinking about how to put it so Mom gets the idea but isn't really clued into it totally.

She's talking to herself while she's rearranging postcards, saying they're not valuable unless they're local, no matter how old they are. She has always collected antiques, but when the house got so full there was hardly any room to walk, Dad said she had to sell them. So she rented a stand at the Dragon and set up her business. When she pauses, I begin, "If there were guns around, and some kids got them and shot them, but no one knew about it, that sure would be bad news."

"Hmmm." She continues rearranging, not looking up, like she hasn't really heard me.

"Because they could shoot something besides a target if they were just fooling around."

She glances up. "There shouldn't be guns around, no matter what. Try telling that to your blockheaded dad. I've always despised them. He knows that.

"Once, when I was a little girl, my father went hunting, and then on the way home he picked me up. I don't know where we were going, but I rode in the back of the truck, and I kept hearing these little sounds. So I pulled back a burlap bag, and there were these bunnies, these poor little half-shot up, half-dead bunnies. Suffering horribly, crying out in agony, all of them dying horrible, painful deaths. I'll never forget it. Tim knows that. He shouldn't be pushing me on this, but he is. I won't take it. He'd better know that."

"Dad doesn't have guns in the garage anymore," I say quickly.

She comes back with, "That's something, but he hasn't gotten rid of them, I bet."

"Wonder where he keeps them?"

She doesn't answer. She's moving on to the silver jam spoons, the ones that are shaped like leaves with flowers around them. She's polishing them, and she says, "See, you don't polish all the tarnish off these lovely things. You leave the tarnish in the creases to give depth and show off the pattern. When you use these, you are using sculpture. See that?"

I nod. "If Dad didn't hide the guns really well, someone

could get them and shoot them. Someone could maybe shoot Bentley."

She looks up at me. "Well, let's hope that doesn't happen."

I'm not going to flat out tell her. Mike and Johnny are horrible, but there's plenty they could tell that I did, like eat a whole package of Oreos and then throw up and lie that I didn't know where the package went. It's not as bad as shooting guns when you're not supposed to and trying to kill Bentley, but still. . . .

"If Dad had the guns hidden but they found them and shot at Bentley, what would you do?" She's looking at me. I turn around with my back to her, like I've really suddenly become terribly interested in the pile of *Country Gentleman* magazines. When Mom tries, she can look straight into my bones.

"I'd skin them alive," she says. That's her normal threat. But then she asks, "Did someone find the guns? Did someone shoot at Bentley?"

I don't want to actually lie, so I shrug. It's a body-lie. She's watching me, just me. My back is turned, but I glance over my shoulder. She's not messing with the spoons or anything, and she's not paying attention to the lady who's looking at her painted washboards. She's just looking at me. In a tone that would sound like Edgar if her voice were as low as his, she demands, "What's going on here, Halley? What do you know? Where are those guns?"

I bend closer to one of the magazines. On the cover there's a lady, and I start to read aloud about her.

"You turn around right now, Halley, and tell me—
where are those guns?"

I'm surprised. I didn't really intend to tell her. I just
wanted her to think about it. "They could be around
here or anywhere. There's a lot of places to put stuff." I
turn around when she doesn't say anything else, and I'm
just in time to see her marching out of the stand. She's
going toward Edgar's. I run out of the stand and try to
catch up with her, but she's moving so fast I have to
keep running.

"Edgar won't know about them. He won't know
where they are."

"Oh, yes, he will." She gives me a look. "Nothing
goes on around here that Edgar doesn't know about. If
they're around, he'll know where they are."

I'm very nervous as she storms into the warehouse.
Edgar just happens to be scooting toward us. He's coming down the main aisle toward his desk, but he doesn't
stop when he gets to us, he just zooms by. At his desk,
using his two cane-sticks, he propels himself onto his
chair with a fluidlike glide that's so smooth, it looks like
he has springs in his butt.

Mom stations herself in front of his desk, and he
slowly turns his huge face toward her, his bulging eyes
settling upon her with a glare. I half expect her to take
a step backwards. Seated at his desk, deformed or not,
Edgar looks extremely powerful.

"Where are they?" Mom demands. Edgar can see she's
angry. Actually, no one could miss it. "The guns! Where
are they?"

His scowl goes from her to me and then back to her. "Back corner," he growls.

Mom doesn't say another word, not "thank you," or anything. She just wheels and heads toward the back, demanding as she goes, "Where, Halley? Show me!" I lead down the dark aisle to the back corner, feeling like what I once heard Uncle Canute call "the worm that chewed the cathedral beam."

In the back she sees them, and she looks like she's not only angry, but is shocked. They're just standing there, propped against the wall, but she approaches them almost timidly, as though they could go off any second and kill us. When she gets to them she reaches out her hand, but then quickly pulls it back. Looking at me doubtfully, she asks, "Are they loaded?"

For some reason I'm finding it difficult to look at her. "I don't think so. You load this kind right before you shoot it. They wouldn't be sitting there loaded."

Suddenly I realize something that I haven't known before—it's not just that she doesn't like them. She's afraid of them. She's afraid to even touch them.

I'm not afraid of them. I want to shoot them. Just now and then, to see if I can hit anything. Maybe just a can, or a big round target. I imagine myself holding one of them against my shoulder, slowly raising it to aim, and sighting along the long barrel as though it's a part of me. I squeeze the trigger and feel the kick, see the fire fly out the muzzle. Maybe, if my aim is good, a can goes *zing!*

With a resolute look, Mom begins grabbing them, one

by one. "They're not very heavy." She sounds surprised.

I'm surprised to see that she is actually touching them. "Where are you going to put them? What are you going to do?"

"What I should have done in the first place," she snaps. She's having a hard time getting the fourth one without dropping the other three.

"I'll take it," I offer.

"No you will not!" she exclaims. "You will not touch any of them."

She gets her arms around all four of them, and then we go out, right past Edgar. He looks up as she goes past, and I'm not sure, but it seems like there might be just the hint of a smile on his face. It's a fleeting change in his look, nothing like a real smile, and it's gone so fast I can't be sure that I actually saw it. I've never seen him smile before.

Out of the Dragon, Mom marches. I look around for Kirk, but I don't see him. The few people who are working at their stands or unloading trucks don't seem to notice as she heads up the creek path. I'm thinking, why is she taking them home? What's she going to do, put them in the car and then take them some place and sell them?

The path by the creek winds and dips, becomes level, and then steep again. At the steep places the creek rushes down, and then where there's level ground it settles in pools. Halfway up Mom leaves the path, walks to the edge of the deepest, largest pool, and hurls the guns to the ground.

I wince when the long, graceful forms slam to the ground, remembering how carefully Dad handled them, how he described the crafting of their meticulously curved locks and their beautifully carved stocks, with the finials and patch boxes and names proudly engraved on the long, octagonal barrels.

"Let him find them here," Mom says, and she picks up the Beck. I'm horrified as soon as I see what she's planning to do. All of me wants to shout, "No!" as the Beck flies through the air and plunges into the deep, still water. I watch in horror as the water settles back over where it went in. Before I look around, the smooth bore is flung past me. Then the Lehigh. Last, the most beautiful one, the one Dad sounds the most happy when he talks about it, the Dickert.

They're gone. There's only water eddying above them. She wipes her hands together like she has to clean them of something horrible.

Inside of me it's like my heart is pounding against a stone, and all of me will soon be broken in two. I feel it's my fault, and I want to say things like, "Dad will never forgive you." But I can't. Mom doesn't say anything, either.

When we get home the boys are there, and they want to go to McDonald's for supper, but Mom says, "No, we're going to open a can of soup and have a sandwich. Things are going to be different around here."

The boys look at me, and I look at the floor. They motion to me and head for the patio. Mike has the swing, and Johnny the chaise. I go to the hammock.

Mike hisses, "Told, didn't you!" before I even sit down.

"No, I didn't," I shoot back at him. "She guessed."

"Oh, that's great!" Mike exclaims. "Just great! Thanks, you crappy little brat. Now we're in a big mess!"

"You shot at Bentley. You went too far."

"We weren't trying to kill your stupid Bentley," Johnny says. "We were just fooling around."

"It doesn't matter now," Mike says.

"You were too trying to kill her! I saw the bullet almost hit her. You're both rotten!"

"You're a stinking snoop," Mike says. "You shouldn't have been up there! What we do is none of your business! Everything would've been okay if you had kept your nose out of it!"

"Yeah, everything would be fine, and Bentley would be fine, too, fine and dead!"

"What're we going to do?" Johnny moans.

Mike's quiet for a moment. "Maybe we'll just wait. See what Dad says when he comes home. He'll be home tonight."

To me he says, "What did she say, Worm Puke?"

I'm miserable and I feel like kicking him. So I smile. Not a real smile, just a little fake smile that's supposed to make them madder. "She didn't *say* anything."

They look at me suspiciously, and I glare back.

"If she didn't say anything, what did she do?" Johnny asks. Both of them look at me with narrowed eyes, like they expect me to go on, but they can just wait. I'm not going to tell them.

Finally they get up and go into the kitchen, and I

follow. Mom's slamming stuff from the dishwasher onto the counter. They just walk through slowly to get a feel for how mad she is. They don't say anything. As they pass she glares at them, and as soon as the glare hits they speed up and head out of the house. I'm behind them.

"You really did it!" Mike spits back at me. "You really, really did! Get away! We don't want you with us. Don't you dare follow us, not one step!"

I scoop up Bentley. "I'm not following you. I'd never follow you."

They're going to the Dragon by way of the creek. I zip down the street and head through town, running so I get there before they do.

When I arrive, I'm out of breath and panting. Kirk's sitting in Akers's truck, shifting the gears. "C'mon," I call to him, not stopping. He jumps down from the truck and catches up to me, loping alongside.

I stop just long enough to get my breath and gasp out, "To the warehouse before the boys get there. They'll go in the back door. We have to listen."

We race in past Edgar and head down the aisle to the back. When we're close to where the guns were, I duck down a side aisle and hunch down, motioning for Kirk to do the same. "What's going on?" he whispers.

I'm still panting from running and I can't talk much. "The guns. Mom got them and took them and threw them in the creek!"

Kirk looks at me, completely shocked. "Your mother! She threw them in the creek!"

"Yeah!" I'm still out of breath.

He gives a low whistle.

"Shhhhh!" I tell him.

"You told on them, that they were shooting?" It's not really a question.

"No. But she guessed, and she went and got them. I was looking for you. Where were you? She just marched right in the warehouse, past Edgar, and got them. Then she took them and threw them in the creek. It was awful! Dad's going to—I didn't want her to do it."

Kirk has this deadly serious look, like I just told him my mother robbed a bank. He's thinking and then he says, "Maybe . . . I don't think they were going to shoot Bentley. They were just . . . your dad . . ."

We hear the end door open, and I motion him to be quiet. First, from Johnny, "They really are gone!"

Then we hear Mike using his worst swear words.

"Gone!" Johnny repeats.

More swearing from Mike.

Kirk looks at me, signals, and we both begin to creep quietly toward the front and out of the warehouse. As we pass, Edgar looks up from his books and growls, "Play outside."

We duck past him out the door and slump down on the porch. "Mike's so furious!" Kirk exclaims.

In a few minutes Mike and Johnny come up the main aisle of the warehouse to the desk where Edgar is working. "Could you tell us where the guns are?" Mike asks.

Edgar's response is a deep, grunted, "No."

"Edgar knows where they are," I whisper to Kirk. "At least he knows Mom took them."

"He doesn't know what she did with them." Kirk sounds like he's defending Edgar. "Edgar always says you shouldn't ever tell anybody anything, you shouldn't even tell your left hand what your right hand is doing."

"Yeah, like he never tells you anything about yourself."

Kirk says, "After you left those two men with accents came around again and asked where Edgar was."

I'm just looking at him. "Did you tell them?"

"No. They asked Doug, you know, the truck driver Harry's son, but I was inside, listening. Doug told them he didn't know."

"He was lying, wasn't he? He knew, didn't he?"

"Yeah. When Edgar heard they were still around, he was really mad. He told me to tell them to go to a really hot place if they come around again."

"Did he mean it, or was he kidding?"

"Edgar never kids."

Mike and Johnny come out past us, and when they see me they demand, "Okay, where are they?"

I don't know where my answer comes from. "Sleeping with the fishes." Kirk whirls around with his eyes wide. Mike lunges toward me and stops with his face a few inches from mine.

"I hope you don't mean what I think you mean."

At that instant I remember where I heard it. "You saw *The Godfather* on TV."

They look horrified. "You didn't!" Mike exclaims.

Johnny says, "Not her, Mom. Mom said she'd throw

them in the creek, remember? I bet she did." For once Mike is too shocked to say anything.

They're towering over Kirk and me. I'm kind of glad Edgar's just inside the door.

"It's your fault," I hiss at them. They glance in Edgar's direction.

"No, it isn't!" Mike snarls. "It's yours, all yours! And everything that's going to happen because of it is your fault, too."

A shudder goes through me, even though I try to stop it.

8

Dad comes home, and he doesn't even say hello. He just walks in and goes up to the bedroom to change and unpack. Then he comes down and sits in front of the TV with his newspaper.

Mike and Johnny are hovering around like they're waiting for the world to end. But, surprisingly, they don't start right in and tell him anything.

Mom doesn't say anything, either. It's like each one thinks that if the other one isn't going to say anything, they aren't, either. Mom finishes the ironing and goes upstairs to work on her computer.

There's a show on TV we all like and we're watching it. Dad says, like he's talking to us because he should, "So, kids, what did you do while I was gone?"

"I went fishing with Kirk," I tell him.

"Catch anything?"

"Nah."

"I got a Tennessee Walking Stick in a jar," Mike says. "Want to see it?"

"Tomorrow," he answers. "We only have this weekend before school starts, and that garage is a mess. Tomorrow we'll get to some of the yard work and clean the garage, but maybe after we get that done we can go out for a while."

I know what he means, shooting. At first I expect Mike and Johnny to tell him. They'll just come out and say, "We can't go shooting because Mom threw the guns in the creek." But they don't.

The guns being in the creek is like this huge subject that, even though it's sitting on us, is so big it's suffocating us. We're making polite talk out from underneath its edges.

After a while Mom calls down for us to start our showers and get ready for bed. A few minutes later Dad says to the boys, "We have to get up early if we're going to get that garage done."

Everything's so stiff. We each go in where Mom's working on the computer and give her a kiss. Then we go down and kiss Dad. We can keep our lights on for a half hour to read, but then we have to turn them off and say our prayers. That's when Mike and Johnny always get Boots's picture out. They look at it with their "This little light of mine" flashlights.

I'm saying to God, "Please, please make it turn out okay! I'm not going to pray about anything else. It's all such a mess. You have to figure it out."

The lights are out, and there are a few minutes of quiet. Then the air is torn by a shrill, "WHAT!" It's very loud, from the boys' room, louder than anything I've ever heard from them.

"Why!" Johnny wails.

It's a horrible sound, and I feel like covering my ears so I don't have to hear it.

Mom's racing toward their room from her computer. Dad's at the bottom of the stairs. "What?" he calls up. I move out to the hall and stand where I can see into their room, but I'm also standing where I can get away quickly by running down the stairs and out of the house.

Mike's holding the microscope, and Johnny has the frame. Their faces are totally shocked, and tears are beginning to flow down their cheeks. What I really want to do is run to my bed and jump in and hide with my covers around my ears, but I have to force myself to stand there making sure I have a path to escape.

Mom's reaching for the picture frame. Mike tries to put it behind his back, but she grabs his arm and pulls it out of his hand. "What's that?"

He points at me and screams, "The monster! She's a monster!"

Mom's reading my note, "'If you shoot Bentley, I'll burn this.' Shoot Bentley? What's the 'this' that's going to get burned? What's going on here?" She looks from him to me.

I'm ready to race out of the house and never, ever come back. She looks down at the note and demands again, "What's going on? What can't you have back?"

Dad has started to climb the stairs and he comes up behind me, blocking my escape route.

Johnny's crying and he shrieks, "Our mother! She took our mother. Our picture!"

Mom echoes blankly, "Your mother?"

"What on earth!" Dad exclaims.

"I'll kill you," Mike screams at me.

Mom turns to him. "Don't you ever say anything like that again!"

Dad rushes past her to Mike. "What is this?" He's looking from one of us to the other.

I'm very frightened, but I have to try. "They shot at Bentley, so I took their picture."

He turns to me, angry and confused. "Shot? And what's this about their mother? Her picture?"

"Boots. They look at her picture every night, but they can't hurt Bentley! No one can! I don't care!" I'm crying.

"We weren't going to shoot her!" Johnny shouts at me.

Mom turns to Dad, furious. "See what you've done! You and your stupid guns! See!"

Dad's looking daggers at all of us. He storms out of the room, but in the hall turns and faces the boys. "You had a picture of her!" he says in this awful, dead tone.

Mom's voice is quavering. "You will all go to bed immediately. None of you will make a sound! Not one sound for the rest of the night! If I hear one sound from any of you, I will not be responsible for what I do." Her fists are clenched.

I glide into my room and onto my bed. Immediately it occurs to me that as soon as Mom and Dad are gone, Mike and Johnny will come in and beat me up. As soon as I think of that, I creep quietly out of bed and look in my desk drawer for tacks to put around.

Downstairs Mom's screaming at Dad. "You brought all this on yourself."

From him, "Oh, put a lid on it. I've had a long day and I don't need to hear this."

"Well, you're going to hear it. Those boys got your

stupid guns while you were gone, and they were shooting them!"

Dad doesn't even sound surprised. He just sounds dull. "I didn't think they'd do that. They let me down." Loud sniffling comes from Mike and Johnny's room.

Mom adds, "I can't believe they had that woman's picture!"

"She is their mother," Dad cuts in.

"Oh is she!" Mom explodes. "Then why am I the one who does their wash, and feeds them, and cleans up after them, if she's their mother! Why am I the one who makes them do their homework! That's for mothers to do! If she's their mother, she can do it. This is insane! I can't take it anymore!"

"I'll talk to them tomorrow about getting the guns," Dad says.

"You don't need to do that," Mom says. "They're gone!"

There's a long silence. I'm holding my breath.

And then his voice, cold with controlled fury. "Gone? Where?"

"None of your business!"

He raises his voice. "Where? You didn't sell them!"

"I'll never tell you!"

I'm waiting for one of the boys to call down, "She put them in the creek," but they don't. From their room the only thing I hear is sniffling and an occasional muffled sob.

9

I have awful dreams, and the next morning when I wake up, at first I think life is good because I am out of the dreams, but as soon as I'm really awake I know my real life is worse.

No one's talking or laughing. It's horrible. Mom's vacuuming, jabbing the vacuum forward and then yanking it back like she's stabbing the room. Her mouth is clamped in a thin, grim line.

Mike and Johnny, when they come down, sit on the opposite side of the room from me and turn on the TV without a word.

When Dad comes down he's dressed, and he doesn't go into the kitchen for breakfast. He just slams out the door. Mike and Johnny exchange looks, then get up and go out after him. I see them walking toward the creek and I start to follow.

Mike turns around. "She's coming." Dad glances back.

"We don't want her," Mike says. He turns and calls to me, "Go away. We don't want you."

"Let her alone," Dad says to him. They're walking along the creek, looking for the guns. I know exactly where they are, and they'll never just see them. They're in a deep part.

I think of telling them, but then I see Bentley sort of

following us up along a high bank and I change my mind. I don't even think of her most of the time, but she's always with me.

Every now and then Mike or Johnny throw a hateful look back at me. Dad's walking close to the creek, scanning carefully as he walks. When he gets to the place where they are, he looks and then goes right on by.

I have to force myself not to say, "There, see? Look closer." But instead I pick up Bentley and wrap her around my face, cooing in her ear, "No one is ever going to hurt you." Dad levels a gaze right at me, and I think he's going to say something, but he doesn't.

We're almost at the Dragon, and Kirk sees us. He's coming in our direction. I'm waiting for Mike to say, "There's your scrawny little wimp, twerp, penny-dog friend," but he doesn't.

I go off with Kirk, and the first thing he says when we're alone is, "How'd it go?"

"Horrible! Dad's furious because he knows Mom threw the guns in the creek. Mom was already angry because of them. The boys found my note, and they hate me. Mom and Dad know they had Boots's picture and they're angry about that. Everyone in my family is mad at everyone else."

"Are you going to tell him where the guns are?"

"No."

"I was talking to Edgar about it last night."

"What'd he say?"

"Nothing. Just that families can sometimes have wars like countries, and then they can destroy each other like countries."

A little while later I'm on the way back up to the house, and I see Dad and the boys going along the creek with Edgar's big magnet on a fishing rod. They're letting it down into the water and then reeling it up. Johnny's carrying a garbage bag, and they're putting all kinds of metal things they've pulled up into it, old cans, rusty screwdrivers, pieces of twisted metal. Soon they'll be at the place where the guns are. I stay way back, but I'm sort of following and watching.

They know I'm there, and every now and then Mike or Johnny glances at me and makes a face, but no one says anything.

When they get to the dark pool where the guns sank in, they lower the magnet. "Got something," Dad says. The boys lean out to see.

"Heavy." He turns the reel. Slowly the magnet breaks the surface with the barrel of the Dickert stuck to it. Shouts of triumph come from all three of them. It's like they are pulling up pirate gold. I'm thinking, they're happy. Now Mom will be sad.

The guns surface, one by one, covered with silt. From where I'm standing, pretty far away, they look awful. I hear from Johnny, "They won't ever be any good."

Dad looks grim. "Well, we can try. We'll clean them up and then see." He wraps them in a burlap bag and turns toward the Dragon. I'm surprised. Somehow I had imagined him taking them home, but instead he's taking them back to Edgar's.

Later that afternoon Aunt Maribeth calls to see if we're coming over for a picnic, because it's a holiday weekend. Mom tells her we're not, and then she spends hours on the phone telling her why we're not and what a mess the family is in.

We don't go swimming or to a movie or anything. Dad just works in the yard or sleeps or works in his study. Mom has the stand open, and there's a craft show. With so many people I have to help her, and she still needs to hire another person.

Mom and Dad definitely aren't speaking to each other. It's like Edgar says, the house is divided, and each part's a country that's at war with the other.

The boys think they belong on Dad's side, but they have to be on Mom's side sometimes, because the kitchen's in her country, and they like to eat.

I want to talk to Dad about Bentley not getting shot, but I don't know what to say. I'm afraid he hates me. I watch carefully to see if he smiles at the boys more than at me. Mostly what I notice is that he doesn't smile at all.

10

After the holiday weekend, school starts. Everyone in town, almost, goes to the Elkins Christian Academy—even Kirk, because the public school is far away, and not very good.

Always, when summer's over and school begins, I feel like I have been transported to a new world. I have to wear different clothes, talk to different people, do different things, and be a different person.

I'm in the sixth grade, and the good news is that neither Mike nor Johnny are actually right in my school anymore. They're both in junior high, which is only across the courtyard, but at least it's a whole different building.

The bad news is that I'm not in the popular group. The main reason is that I can't do back-bends or flips, and I don't play softball.

Every morning all the popular girls do back-bends and flips in the cafeteria, and every recess every day they play softball. Mom never allowed me to take gymnastics because she said she wanted me to be as tall as possible, and she thinks there's something about gymnastics that messes up your soft-bone cartilage and makes you end up shorter than you would have been.

I'm not good at softball because my hand-eye coordination is a joke.

I do have friends. My best one, Tess, is writing a computer program that plays her new game—chess, with the rules changed so that the queen and the real estate (the castles) are as important as the king.

Even with not being in the popular group, everything is going all right until one of the super pops, the most snooty one, says, "I don't know why all those kids always hang around Halley and Tess. They can't do anything." Then there has to be a war.

We ask Kirk for help in formulating the plan, and it takes a whole lunch recess, but when it's done it's perfect. As soon as it's done, we let our other friends in on it, just a few at a time.

The "can't do anything" comment was aimed at me for striking out twice when I did make an attempt to play softball. Since they made the comment about softball, we're going to attack softball. We're going to steal all the balls and bats.

First, we send carefully chosen raiders to approach the game by twos and threes, just like they want to play. Except that, when they get in position, like lightning they snatch up all the balls and bats. Even the ball and bat being used at the time.

We strike on the last recess. I'm one of the raiders, and while I'm racing away with three bats I give a sweeping glance around to make sure everyone else is successful. As soon as we have all the balls and bats, we tear back to the fort where the rest are waiting.

At first the softball players just stand around looking astonished. They're too surprised to do anything except to make a few automatic, shocked protests. But mostly they're gaping at us with their mouths open. It's perfect.

At the fort we take our positions and wait for them to counterattack. Our fort's the cement stairway that leads into the basement. This particular stairway has a protective stone wall around it so it's easy to defend. It's no accident that real castles are built on high hills, or at least with moats around them. As a fort the stairway is perfect, unless someone thinks of throwing stones in on top of us, but no one would do that.

The players are furious. They come and call us every name they can think of, but we just chant "Nanny, nanny, na, na" at them and do victory dances and make faces.

Tess calls out, "You have to choose your generals, first. Then plan your strategy. You're never going to get anywhere until you do that."

Kirk says to her, "Why are you helping them figure out how to defeat us? They're the enemy. Let them think of how to do it."

They form into several opposing armies and spend the rest of that recess planning. Some of them want to tell the playground monitors, but even the most dedicated ballplayers nix the "tattletale" idea.

The balls and bats are the treasures that we must defend at all cost, like the king in chess. They're deep inside the fort. All of our forces are guarding the walls and entrance, but control of the balls and bats is the key to success.

The thing that makes it so great is that, mingled with all the names and hostility, there's a lot of respect. Suddenly there's a new game to play with balls and bats. And it's soon obvious that some of them are enjoying it.

Their first counterattack is an effort to hand several little kids down from the steps that go into the building above the fort. The little kids are supposed to get in, get the balls and bats, and then run out. But we just capture them as soon as they're let down, and shove them out the entrance. Two of them don't want to leave, but we shove them out, anyway, because we can't trust them not to be traitors.

Some kids stand outside the fort and shout insults instead of actually trying to figure out a way to overpower us and get the stuff back.

We tease them. Tess and I pretend to have mini games of catch. Kirk holds up a bat and says, "Here's a bone, doggy, doggy. Be a good pooch and come in and get it."

Some of them actually swear, but the thing about swear words is, if you say them a few million times, they have no more effect than some ordinary word, like "cow" or "boat."

Getting in and out of the building with the balls and bats is the most critical operation. When recess is over our army lines up with ball-and-bat carriers surrounded by a close formation of defenders. The actual carrier is the smallest one. I'm a defender. We're human shields.

Several defenders are grabbed and shoved, but the playground supervisor, who reads a magazine all recess and only stops reading and stands up when it's time to go in, tells everyone to settle down now, recess is over.

Inside we guard the balls and bats until the players have to sit down. Critical to the plan is that we always leave them last and get to them first.

On the next day, lunch recess, we get a rain of shoes. But the only consequence of that is that the people who throw them are barefoot. We hold up their shoes and tease them with them. When they get them back, all the laces are removed or tied together in a zillion knots, so they have to go into the building walking like they just got home from Kmart.

When several kids arrive at school with bats and balls from home, we confiscate them, too.

We keep the balls and bats for three days, and our fort is defended against wave after wave of attack. Sometimes some of our people are captured, and once a ball. Another time one bat, but never both together.

Three days is as long as any war can last and still be fun. After recess on the third day we simply hand the balls and bats back. A lot of them are actually disappointed. Several say, "You have to keep them till we capture them."

But we just smile to convey the message that, for the moment, we're tired of the game. But if we should ever need to do it again, we will.

I've won so much respect that I can play ball some-

82

times, even clumsily, and no one will make fun of me. Now and then I actually hit it and get home.

A girl who lives up the street offers to teach me to do back-bends and flips. She starts by having me go over four beanbags. I have to do it where Mom can't see until I'm really good. She'd say something like, "I don't care how good you are, you still have to wear a helmet."

11

A week later during recess I'm sitting grumbling because there's a hole in my shoe and stones are getting in and hurting my foot so I can hardly walk. Kirk goes past, and when he sees what's wrong he says, "Come inside, I'll make you a cardboard shoe sole." He likes to think of ways to fix things. He's like Edgar: If something doesn't work the usual way, then he thinks of a different way.

It's a golden September day, and everyone, even Mrs. Oht, who almost never leaves the room, is outside. Kirk traces the sole of my shoe on cardboard, and then he starts rummaging around in the cabinet for scissors and more cardboard. "Hurry up," I tell him. "Recess'll be over soon, and Tess and I are making grass bracelets. Mom'll get me new sneakers tonight."

He can't find scissors that are heavy enough to cut the cardboard, but then he remembers the huge scissors in Mrs. Oht's desk. He has to use both hands to cut the cardboard with them.

I'm terribly impatient, but he can't go any faster. "I hope Mom takes me tonight. Since she's mad at Dad and he's mad at her, I never know . . ." I don't finish the sentence, because I don't like to think about bad stuff at school.

I'm sitting on the table in the front of the room. Kirk's the only one I ever talk to about Mom and Dad. Tess doesn't even know. There's a glass jar of goo on the table with a brush in it. I pull up the brush and look at it, some kind of green, sticky gunk. The table's covered with newspaper, so I brush a few strokes of it on the paper to see what it is.

Kirk glances at it. "What's that?"

I just shrug.

"Here," he says, "try this." I stick my foot into the shoe.

"That's great, thanks." He's already out the door.

Outside, I scrape my foot on some gravel and it doesn't hurt. It really works.

Before I even have enough long grass for my bracelet, the buzzer sounds and we have to go in. The whole recess is wasted.

As we settle down we begin to notice that Mrs. Oht is standing in the front of the room, quivering. Her eyes look watery, and the little feather thing that she has stuck in her hair is jiggling. No one is particularly surprised. She gets upset over everything, and she quivers all the time.

Jiggling like she's doing, in a normal person, would be a sign of some horrible thing, maybe the world was going to end, and she had to give us instructions about our flight to another planet. But with Mrs. Oht it's probably something like there's a spider in the chalk tray.

She starts to speak, and the quivering gets worse,

worse than we've ever seen. Maybe the world is going to end. It might be something serious. She tries to get out a sentence, but she can only manage, "Who . . . ?" She turns to the table behind her and points to the green gunk. Her hand, her whole arm is shaking, and her voice when she tries to speak, warbles wildly. "Who did this?"

Did what, is the first thing I think.

Her voice reaches a screech. "Who was in here! Who touched this! Who" —then her voice sinks to a low, horrified tone— "opened this bottle and smeared all of this over the table?"

I feel a horrible, sinking, oops! Mega-oops! I don't dare look guilty. My gaze has to be steady, and it has to proclaim innocence. I'm looking blank, but my mind is racing. Kirk knows I did it. Does anyone else? I don't think so.

Her bright black beady little eyes rake the room. Everyone stirs nervously, so I do, too. Everyone looks guilty. That's good. Everyone has done something that could set her off. Some days all it takes is breathing.

Kirk is three rows over and back several seats, where I can't see him unless I turn around to look.

No one says anything. "Who?" she demands again. "You will confess!"

She looks like she's going to kill whoever did it, that's definite. And she expects them to confess? Is she crazy? Yes, she is! I'd just as soon confess to some major crime, like racketeering or disturbing the mayhem. The way she looks, the punishment would be the same.

I look for an avenue of escape. The window's open. Kirk won't tell, but someone else—no one else was in the room, but—maybe someone was looking in the window, or walking past and I didn't see them, and they'll tell. Then I'm out of here.

I'll fly out the window, right through the screen. It isn't far to the ground. But, I don't think I can dash past her fast enough. She'll catch me. I could go through the audio room and out the door. I'll run the whole way home and never go back again. Ever.

I'll go to public school or Mom can teach me. She can make me add up the receipts from her stand and subtract her expenses and multiply her hours by something or other. She can teach me to do it as fast as a computer.

Dad teaches history in college. He could tell me the history of guns while he's working on them up in the fire hall. That's where they are now. He's always up there with Mike and Johnny working on them.

If I didn't go to school, Mom could tell me about the history of pottery and books. I can learn just about anything from Mom and Dad, or from The Learning Channel or The Discovery Channel. I wouldn't have to stay here in school and lose my life.

Mrs. Oht launches into her shame speech. She's trying to sink whoever did it with a rock of guilt. "None of you has the courage? No one has the decency? To do something like this and just leave it . . . ! And then to compound the sin by not confessing? God knows. The God who sees inside of you knows. He's looking at your soul!

"You'll burn in the searing fires of Hell if you don't confess and wash your soul clean. Silence is a lie. Our Heavenly Father knows, and your lie is an abomination before Him."

None of what she says bothers me, but I'm worried about Kirk. He's very religious, and he never lies. He doesn't have brothers and sisters, so he never needs to.

While she goes on and on, I just try to concentrate on looking innocent and hoping Kirk won't cave. I can't even turn around and look at him.

I'm sure he will cave. He'll have to. He won't be able to take having her talk about his soul being bad. God's his friend. He talks to Him all the time. I pray, too, but I'm not thinking of God at the moment. I'm trying to save my skin.

"I'm going to go around the room and ask each one of you to swear upon the sacred Word that you did not do this. If you can't swear to our Lord that you didn't do it, then you must confess. Remember, you aren't speaking to me. You are speaking to God. You cannot lie before your Creator.

"Start, Jeff. Say, 'I swear before our Lord that I did not touch the green ink, and I do not know who did.' Say that."

Jeff says, "I swear before the, uh . . ."

Mrs. Oht repeats, looking disgusted, "I swear before our Lord that I did not touch the green ink, and I do not know who did."

"I swear to God I didn't touch it, and I don't know who did."

"No!" she screams. Then she grabs some chalk and

writes it on the board. "That! Swear to that! Exactly. Don't leave out one word! Not one word!"

Jeff reads it.

"Next, Corinne!" It goes down the first row and is coming to me. One boy, a girl, and then me. I could confess and make this terrible thing stop. It's horrible. Kids all around me are looking dead, like they're not even in their own bodies, because it's too dangerous.

I could jump up and run out, shouting on my way, "I did it, so you can stop all this now." Or, I could confess and just sit there and be killed.

I'm trying to decide which one to do when it gets to me, and I read it in the same tone as everyone else. "I swear before our Lord that I did not touch the green ink, and I do not know who did."

I'm thinking I could just die or something from telling such a lie. But my words are done, and the boy behind me is saying them. I take a breath. I'm still breathing. I'm still alive.

Mrs. Oht's little beady black eyes are raking each of us as we speak, trying to spot the lie in someone's shaky voice or nervous look.

Soon she'll be at Kirk. He either has to betray me or tell a lie. I'm ready to run. I should run to save him from making either choice. It's the same decision all over again that I have to make. I'm slow in making it, and the strange, dead progression of denials comes to him while I hold my breath.

"I swear before our Lord . . ." he goes, and the lie pours forth from him like a blessing. Then beyond him, on and on, through the whole room as the innocent proclaim the truth.

We spend the rest of the morning, each of us writing one hundred and fifty times, "I will not touch things without permission." One girl begins to cry because she says holding the pencil for so long makes her fingers hurt.

Mrs. Oht is no longer angry. It's like her great swell of rage has gone, and she's an empty shell. She's standing before us, but she's not really even there.

When we all go down to lunch we're looking at each other, kind of shocked. I look at everybody the same way, except Kirk, whom I don't look at at all.

But after lunch we're outside, and when I see him alone I kind of walk close to him and ask, "Why didn't you tell?"

"She's nuts," he says.

"Yeah, but to swear to God!"

Kirk just shrugs. "God's smarter than that."

12

Kirk and I are in the warehouse, and I'm talking to him while I look at my picture and try to figure out how I can get three hundred dollars. It's after school, a hot afternoon in late September, with the sun slanting the same way it does in the middle of winter.

Kirk and I haven't mentioned Mrs. Oht or the green ink. It's just something we had to do, like if we were hostages and had to lie to keep each other alive.

It's dark in the warehouse, even with the light that comes through the few rickety, dirty windows. I'm telling him, "Mom says she shouldn't have married Dad, and Dad told Johnny he doesn't do well in relationships. They don't talk to each other unless they have to, and then when they do talk, it's mean."

Kirk's bouncing a paddleball. I tell him, "I can do that seven hundred and ninety-four times without missing." He nods appreciatively. Mike or Johnny would say something like, "I can do that all afternoon and all night and for the next week without missing."

"We really shouldn't be in here," Kirk says. "Edgar says he doesn't want kids messing around."

"That sounds grumpy."

Kirk looks at me thoughtfully. "He has spinal arthritis.

The doctor told him his spine wasn't meant to do the things he makes it do. It has to do what legs and arms would do if he had them."

Saturday night I'm in bed thinking about the mess my family is in. I pray about it for a long while, and then I'm ready to go to sleep, but Bentley isn't there. I feel around the bed for her. She isn't even on the bed.

That's not too unusual. She usually comes to bed with me, but sometimes she has other business to take care of, like going to her litter box. Or she's even outside sleeping on the hammock. Sometimes when I've been running around all day and she's been following me, she gets so tired she goes to sleep under a bush. Usually she's in the laundry room on the clean wash, and all I have to do is meow, and then she wakes up and comes to bed. But sometimes when she's really out of it, I have to actually go down and pick her up. Then she's so tired, she's practically limp.

I meow several times, but she doesn't come. So I slide out of bed, stick my toes in my slippers, and go down to get her. I have to have her in bed with me so I can fuzz her with my fingers. I can't go to sleep without her.

She isn't in the laundry room. Mom's cleaning out the refrigerator, and Dad's working at the dining room table. Mom doesn't even notice me, but Dad says, "It's time you were in bed."

"I can't find Bentley." I open the door, lean out, meow, and wait. No Bentley. So I start looking in other places.

Mom says from inside the refrigerator, "She's probably

outside. Cats like nice fall nights like this when it's a full moon."

I go to the door and call. I call and call, but she doesn't come.

"Look under the bed or something," Dad says irritably. "She wouldn't be out this late, full moon or not."

Mom gives him a spiteful look. "Like you would know!"

I begin crying, and Mom shoots at Dad, "Can't you help her? I can't do everything."

"I'll find her," I say quickly, and I race around the whole house, looking everywhere, under beds and in closets, behind the refrigerator, out in the garage.

Mom leaves the refrigerator and starts hunting, too. She calls upstairs, "Mike, Johnny, help find Bentley, or no one'll ever get to sleep."

There's a pause, and then Mike calls down, "There's something white out in the garden. It looks like her. I think she's dead."

From me there comes a tremendous scream. Dad's up, striding across the family room and out the door. I can see him out the window crossing the yard to the garden. Mike and Johnny race down the stairs and tear past me. Mom goes out on the deck, but I just stand in the kitchen. I'm screaming. In slow motion I move to the back door.

Dad comes back across the yard, and as soon as I see his face, I know. He looks at Mom, horribly shocked, and then at me. "Dead!" Just one word, but it's like a million words because of all it means to me.

"What!" Mom runs past him to the door and looks out. Then she turns back to him. "Bentley! Are you sure! She's out there, dead!"

He nods. Mike and Johnny come back in.

"Who? How?" Mom begins.

Dad turns slowly to the boys. "Shot!"

Mom slumps to the sofa, sobbing. Mike and Johnny start talking fast. "We didn't, we wouldn't, we . . ."

Inside of me there is such pain! I'm flailing around the family room and sobbing, but nothing will stop the pain.

Dad walks slowly out to the garage and comes back in with a shovel.

"What!" Mom exclaims.

He says, not looking at anyone, "She has to be buried. Animals could come and drag her off. Dogs, other . . ." His voice trails off.

Mom's still sobbing, but she jumps up and runs to the back door. "Wait! Wait a minute! You can't bury her. Not yet! No!" Dad turns around. "Halley has to see her."

I start to back away. "I don't want to! I can't!"

But Mom puts her arm around me. "You must!"

"No, no, no!"

She is half lifting to hold me up. "If she has to be buried now, you have to see her now. You can't not see her. Things have to be seen exactly the way they are." She has gotten suddenly very calm, and she pushes me out the door and across the patio to the yard.

Ahead in the moonlight are the dark, shadowed forms of old, half-knocked-down corn and huge tomato plants that are rambling out of their cages. All of the garden's dark rows and clumps look like black etchings. In the moonlight, surrounded by all the dark forms, is a patch of white. A still, gleaming form. It is my beloved Bentley, more still than anything. More still than the tomatoes or corn!

I stiffen my legs, plant my feet firmly, and refuse to move one step closer. But even there I can make out the terrible dark wounds in her soft, white fur. I think I can't bear it, but then in an instant I suddenly know—it isn't Bentley. It's the body she used to have, but she is no longer there.

Mom pulls me forward, but I cry, "I see!" Then I turn and run sobbing back to the house.

"No, no! Not dead! She can't be dead! I love her! She loves me!" I run through the house and out again, out the front door and down to the creek path.

Before I get very far, I have to stop, because I'm out of breath from crying. I run and then stop, then run some more. In the moonlight the ripples on the creek are flashing like glittering silver through my tears. I call out to the night, "Bentley! Bentley! Where are you! Don't be hurt! Don't be dead, my beloved friend!"

On and on I race. It's like the thought of death is chasing me, and I'm running to get away from it. But when I get to the Dragon, death is still with me, and there's no place else to run.

Everything is dark and still, all the buildings deserted. I've never seen the Dragon when it wasn't filled with life and light, but now there are only black and silver shadows in the moonlight. Through my sorrow, there comes a sense of wariness. This Dragon is a strange, new territory.

In my mind, things begin to settle. Mike and Johnny shot Bentley, I know that. And they did it because I took Boots's picture. Bentley's dead because of them . . . and me!

At home Dad is digging her grave. He'll put her in it, and the ugly brown earth will fall upon her. It'll fall upon her beautiful white fur that I brushed and petted and picked burrs out of. The dirt will fall on her red wounds. And her bright green eyes will stare lifelessly beneath the dirt. I am completely defeated.

13

I stumble on, down the Dragon's eerily empty street. But then I suddenly become aware of voices. I'm in front of Akers's stand, and the minute I hear them I stop walking and shrink back into the giant shadows made by stacks of orange crates. I stand there very still and listen. One of the voices is Edgar's, coming from the warehouse.

I peep around a crate. Edgar's on the porch, sitting on the old wicker rocker. In front of him, leaning on a post, is Frank, the mechanic. Edgar's gesturing with his two hooked sticks. I listen, straining to hear what they're saying. Something about politics.

Stealthily I turn around and creep to the back of Akers's stand. Then I dash along the backs of the other stands until I'm behind the warehouse. At the door to Kirk and Edgar's living area I pause and look in for a light. Maybe Kirk will be up, or even messing around in the dark. But I don't see him. It's very late. He can go to bed when he wants to, but he's probably sleeping.

I don't want to talk to anyone, anyway. I go on, around to the end door, and reach for the white ceramic knob, turning it slowly. The door opens, and I step in and close it softly behind me.

Tears are flowing down my face and dripping off my chin. I slump in front of my picture and sit hunched with my arms wrapped around my knees.

The warehouse is so dark that I can't really see it. I'm crying softly so they can't hear me out on the porch. I can hear Edgar's and Frank's voices, but I can't make out their words, just that they sound like they are enjoying their argument.

At another time I would think the warehouse, deserted and dark, was creepy. I'd imagine spiders and bugs everywhere, but now it doesn't matter. All I can think, and all I can feel, is pain.

Then it's like God notices, because when the pain is so strong I think I can't take it anymore, the moon suddenly comes flooding through the cobweb-covered windows and is shining on my picture. My picture is suddenly completely illuminated, and I can see it clearly in every detail—the water in endless waves, their motion painted still.

Bentley is dead. I think it has to be a punishment to me. Because I lied. Or maybe something else. Maybe even because of my parents. But why her? She was innocent. She just sat and purred, looking wise and beautiful, and she didn't know anything about defying the laws of God.

I'm there a long while and have sort of gone to sleep when I suddenly awaken to the sound of voices. It's Mom and Dad, and they're outside. They're knocking on Edgar's door, calling, "Edgar, Edgar! Excuse us, Edgar!"

I hear Edgar's gruffer than ever. "Go away!"

There's more knocking, and then Mike and Johnny call, "Kirk, Kirk, are you there? Have you seen Halley?"

"Halley?" from Kirk. "What time is it?"

There's more sound. And now I can hear them very plain. They're inside of Edgar's, just through the wooden wall. If there was a light I could probably see them through the cracks because the wall's just wooden slats that aren't tight together.

Mike says, "Someone shot Bentley. . . ." I've been sleeping and have almost forgotten, but with the words the pain surges back through me again.

"And Halley took off," from Johnny.

"The boys thought she might have come here," Mom says. "We don't want to bother you, but we have to find her."

I'm shivering, even though it isn't cold. I'm curled up in a tight little ball, and I wish they'd just go away. I don't want to be awake. I don't want to think.

But they keep talking and calling.

"Could she be in the warehouse?" Dad suggests. "Is it locked?"

I don't hear any more talk, but there's thumping, and then the door opens up along the wall, not far away.

"If she's here, I know where she'll be," Kirk says. They are approaching; I hear steps and voices.

Quickly I scuttle under a big dresser, and then over to a sofa and under it. Cobwebs, thick and sticky, itch across my face and arms, and I imagine the huge spiders that are sitting on top of me in the dark, trying to figure out where to bite first.

A short distance away from my face I see all their shoes and Edgar's wheels. Kirk, traitor Kirk, says, "She'd be here." They're standing in front of my picture.

"Why . . . ?" Mom asks. "Oh, that picture. She told me about it." Her voice quavers as she exclaims, "Well, if she isn't here, where is she? Where could she be, off in the dark, alone! Who knows what could happen to her!"

"She's here!" Johnny exclaims. "See that?" A flashlight beam shines on the floor in front of my picture, and even I can see it, a wet shoe print.

"She's always here," Kirk says.

"It's wet," from Mike. "She's here."

The flashlight beam shines right in my face. So of course I have to scuttle out at their feet in front of all of them.

I'm out, and all their hands are reaching to me, but I dodge them and rush to my picture. There, I drop and face it, sitting with my arms wrapped around my knees.

Johnny says so loud it's like he wants the spiders to hear, "We're sorry about Bentley!"

I can't help it, but I just start rocking back and forth moaning.

"Why's she doing that?" Mike asks. "It's creepy." He sounds horrified. I'm making long, loud moans.

"Don't you say one word to her!" Mom demands. "Her beloved pet is shot dead, and you threatened to kill it. You have no right to criticize her!"

"Gwen! That will be enough!" Dad exclaims. "You don't know that the boys killed Bentley." He turns to them and asks, with his voice cracking, "You didn't, did you, fellows? You couldn't do anything like that, could you?"

Immediate no's come from Mike and Johnny, but I'm certain that they're lying. The lump in my throat is so big I almost choke, and rage is shaking me like Bentley shook her catnip mouse. I can't believe it, but my arms and legs are jerking, and I'm biting at the air.

Suddenly Edgar hurtles toward me on his platform. He stops just short of running over me and booms out in his deep growl, "Get up, girl. It's only a cat." Then he grabs under my arms with his two sticks and forces me up. With his huge face before me and his bulging eyes glaring, his sticks hold me motionless in a powerful grasp as he bellows, "Only a cat!"

Mom rushes toward me, but he roars, "Back!" flashing her a glare. Then he gives me a slight shake. I can't look anywhere except at him. He roars again, "Only a cat!"

Mom's trying to say something, and Kirk's trying to explain what Bentley meant to me, but I can look only at Edgar. Once, I would have been petrified to have him grasp me, even to come near me, let alone boom at me in his loud voice, but now I'm not. The huge, angular furniture towers all around us in the moonlight, and Edgar, grotesque Edgar, booms at me, and I'm not afraid. Instead, I'm comforted. I'm not afraid.

He still looks frightful, and I'm held motionless by his rods. He's trying to tell me something. It's about loss, something about . . . legs that didn't grow or arms that never were, or pain in the spine. I look at him, and I try to understand.

He lets me go so abruptly that I have to catch myself

to keep from falling over. Mom and Dad each reach out to me, but I evade their grasp and careen toward my picture. At first I hesitate, but then my eyes settle on Mike and Johnny and I reach down behind it and pull out the photo of Boots. Looking right at them I start to tear it. First in half, and then, clasping one half under my arm, I tear again. I tear and tear until each piece is small.

"What's that? What's she—Mommy!" Mike shouts and lunges for me.

Some of the pieces are already stamp sized, and I let them flutter to the wooden floor. Johnny realizes and throws himself on me with a howl, grabbing for the untorn half. But I twist away from him, from everyone, and continue tearing, jerking out of their grasps, shouting the accusation over and over, "You took Bentley from me!"

Mike has got me and he's trying to hold me still with one arm so he can grab. But I continue to dodge and jerk and shred until nothing of the picture remains that shows anything.

Dad exclaims, "What's that?" He grabs me and holds me still until he figures out what I'm tearing and then he releases me with an exclamation of disgust.

"What!" Mom exclaims. She sees and then stands back with a bitter look. Off to one side I catch sight of Edgar gliding away.

As the last pieces flutter to the floor, Mike and Johnny pound on the arm of a leather sofa with their fists. Then, shouting, they run out of the warehouse.

Mom is yelling at Dad, and he's yelling back at her.

They both leave, yelling at each other. Then only Kirk and I are left. Kirk looks at me and shakes his head.

From outside Mom calls, "You come out here now, Halley." As I leave, Kirk is bending down, methodically gathering up the pieces.

14

We go home through the town. Dad first. Then Mom, a lot behind him. Mike and Johnny are way behind them. None of us are together. I'm the farthest behind, not even really with them at all, except that Mom turns around every now and then to make sure I'm coming. It's like we're each one of us so far apart, we're separated by a couple of longitudes. I feel like a captive in chains forced to follow four enemies.

When we're at home Mom doesn't say anything to anyone except me. "It's three A.M. Go to bed, Halley. We'll talk tomorrow." Then she goes to her half of the house, and Dad goes to his.

In the morning I'm deeply asleep when Mom starts shaking me. "Halley, wake up. Halley. I called you an hour ago. I thought you were up. We'll be late for church."

I get up and pull on my dress, socks, and shoes, but I'm not really much awake, even when I stumble out to the car.

"Where's Dad?" Mike and Johnny ask.

Mom is backing down the driveway, and she doesn't answer.

"He's gone," Johnny declares somberly.

"Dad's gone?" I'm a little more awake. "Where!"

"Lakeport," from Mom in a clipped tone.

"Uncle Canute?" Mike asks.

"Yes. He left a note, 'Gone to Lakeport.'" She adds sarcastically, "He can be counted on to hunt up his big brother, Canute, when things get hot."

I'm in the front seat, and Mike and Johnny are in the back. Johnny whispers really low to Mike, "Bet he took the guns with him. He said he was going to."

"I wish we could have them here," Mike says. He's shooting accusing glances at Mom.

"Yeah," Johnny agrees, "it was so much fun."

Mom looks into the rearview mirror and glares at them. She can hear a pin drop in China.

When we're at home after church and changing our clothes, I look out my bedroom window and see the fresh earth scar. That's where Bentley is. She should be with me, on my bed or walking across my bureau, maybe winding around my ankles. I feel a horrible aching sorrow, and I start to cry.

The boys both go past my door and look in. They're like, twitching, but they don't say anything.

Mom calls up, "There are slices of roast beef in the refrigerator if you want a sandwich. I'm going to the Dragon. Halley, you come with me."

I call down through my sobs, "No!"

She's getting things ready to take with her, and she calls back, "It isn't a request. I want to talk to you."

"Talk won't help. It won't make Bentley alive."

She comes up and stands in my doorway. "I know it won't, but we're going to talk, anyway. Come on."

We're going in the car because she has been to an auction and there's a lot of new stuff. When we get to where we should turn off for the Dragon, she keeps going, turning instead onto the road that goes up to Dinky's Bluff. When we get to the top of the bluff she parks the car under the trees.

Dinky's Bluff's a knob of earth that sticks up, kind of like a hill that is flat on top, like a cut-off tree stump. Everyone goes up there to hike and have picnics. On the side of the bluff is a place where there's real clay, good enough for making pottery, and people get buckets full of it to take home and mold into bowls and things. From the top of the bluff you can see for miles.

We can look down on our house, or further out to the Dragon and the town. Way out is the public school, and in the other direction is our school.

Groups of people are hiking up, and several other groups are already there. They're sitting on blankets and lawn chairs, playing games and eating. Mom gets out of the car and just stands leaning against it, looking out to the distance. "I feel so bad about little Bentley," she begins forlornly. "I loved her, too."

I've been crying through the whole drive, and now I begin to sob. "I did everything with her! I can't stand never having her again! I won't ever be able to go to sleep!"

Mom looks up to a big white cloud that's floating right above us. Beyond it there's endless, deep blue sky. She looks like she'll soon cry, too.

"Last night Edgar said she's just a cat! Like she was nothing!"

"Oh," Mom sighs, "that's just Edgar." She's staring at the cloud, not looking at the people or me or anything. We just sit in silence for a long time.

The next time she talks, her voice has changed to an almost happy tone. "I'll always remember what a cute kitten she was. Do you remember how you fed her with a doll's bottle? And she drank from it, too, the little pig, bottle after bottle. They told us she was weaned and she wouldn't drink from a bottle, but you wanted to feed her that way, and she just drank and drank. Canned milk. She loved it. I'd warm it . . ."

We're both crying. She scoots over to where I'm sitting with my arms wrapped around my legs, and puts her arm around me. She's an awkward hugger. I never remember her hugging much, and it's like she thinks that's what she should do, but it's something that isn't right for her.

I let her, because it's nice that she's trying. Actually it's nicer than if she were just doing it because that's what she felt comfortable doing.

I'm sobbing, "Why do they hate me so much? Why did they do it! Why would they kill her? She never did anything to them!"

Mom's beginning to cry so loud other people are looking at us. I get embarrassed easily.

"I don't know, Halley. I thought I knew them, all three of them, Tim and his sons. My sons. They've been with us for so long, eight years. They were six and five when they came. Just little fellows. I felt so sorry for them when Boots left them, and I tried to love them and make it up to them. But I failed! I failed miserably!

"For them to do something so horrible! And what other explanation would there be? No one else would have any reason to do that. They . . . they just got carried away with that shooting or something. . . .

"I've been blaming the guns, but it isn't just them. It goes much deeper than that. You shouldn't have torn up Boots's picture. I didn't even know they had it until you tore it. It shows how little I knew what was going on with them. How did you know they had it?"

I just shrug.

"Well, it's too much for me." She's no longer sobbing. But she looks very sad, and she's staring into space. "Of course your taking their picture gave them no right to shoot Bentley.

"What an awful thing! I can't bear this! When I went to bed last night I thought I could sleep, but I couldn't. I stayed awake all night. Then I thought we'd go to church and pray, and maybe that would help. I didn't listen to the sermon at all, I just prayed and prayed. I'm trying to act normal and follow my usual routine, but for Tim to just take off and leave me here with this! It's like everything is broken, and I'm all alone here with the pieces!

"I don't know what to say to the boys. They must be punished, but I don't know . . . I have to talk to someone. I need someone to help. I may just . . . throw in the towel."

I look at her. "You mean . . . ?" I can't say the word "divorce" because even when I think it, there are like electrical shocks that go all along my arms and legs and body.

We're quiet, but she's hugely sighing, and she's about to cry again. "I don't know. It's something I never thought would happen to us. Such a terrible thing—divorce, a sacred pledge broken.

"I think that's one of the problems with Mike and Johnny. Boots just dropped them and took off. She promised to come back and get them, but she never did! She didn't even write. They looked and looked for a letter in the mailbox. They were so hopeful, and the looks on their faces when I went through the mail and there wasn't anything, day after day! Every time the phone rang for a year afterward they listened hopefully! I could see it. You were too young to know, but it was terrible how those little boys suffered. I tried to take her place, but I know now that I failed."

She's like she will go on and on, but I practically scream at her, "I don't want to feel sorry for them! They killed Bentley! It wasn't her fault! It wasn't!"

Mom's getting up and brushing off the dried grass. "I know. We have to get down to the Dragon and open the stand."

15

The next day is Monday. After school I'm in the warehouse sitting in front of my ocean picture, and Kirk comes in. He holds something out to me. "I put this together. Want to see it?"

"What? Oh, Boots's picture. No, I don't want to see it. I don't like her, and I don't like Mike, and I don't like Johnny."

Kirk drops down beside me and leans against the leather club chair. "Edgar says that hate is an acid that burns the pot that holds it more than the person it's poured upon."

"So what!"

"I think he means if you think a lot about not liking someone, you could get ulcers."

"Who cares!"

Kirk's practically waving Boots's picture in front of my face. He has glued all the pieces together on a cardboard backing. I glance at it. Actually, with all the tear lines it looks like a puzzle, a picture puzzle. I can see he wants me to admire his work, but I can't.

"She's a hideous witch. I don't know why they even care about her. She left when they were so little. I wonder why she never came or called."

He sighs and puts Boots's picture down on his other side, like he's afraid if he puts it near me I'll grab it and tear it up again.

"What are you going to do with it?"

He just shrugs.

I don't feel like talking, and Kirk's always content to sit quietly until I think of something to do. He's trying to fix a yo-yo so it goes up and down right.

I'm thinking of how big a mess my life is in, and there's a lump in my throat. After a long while when I'm sure I can talk without crying, I say to him, "I don't think Dad'll ever come back. Mom thinks that, too."

Kirk drops the yo-yo in his pocket and starts trying to lock all of his fingers together. They keep coming apart. I could show him how to do it with none of them coming apart, but I don't care enough to bother.

"Dad likes living with Uncle Canute. Mike said to Johnny this morning that he'll stay there because he likes it so much." Tears start down my face. I'm thinking that I'll have to get up and leave because I don't want Kirk to know I'm crying. But the warehouse is pretty dark, and he's not really noticing me. He's busy trying to get his fingers stuck together.

I just let my nose run so he won't hear me sniffing. "Dad went to Uncle Canute after he got divorced from Boots. That's where Mom met him. I know he'll never come back." I'm sure I'll be really crying in a minute, so I get up and leave in a hurry. Kirk doesn't say anything, and he just knows I don't want him to come along. That's the kind of friend he is.

* * *

Later, at home, Mom's in the kitchen, and Mike and Johnny are hanging around. They keep walking through, but she doesn't say anything to them or even tell them to do something, like put the peanut butter jar away, or pick up all the sofa pillows.

Finally, when she hasn't talked to them or looked at them for a long time, Mike just comes out with, "We didn't shoot Bentley!" Her eyes settle on him for an instant, then she looks away.

"We didn't! Someone else—maybe Gary or Eddie Sower. They have guns, and they're mean. Their mother's always shouting stuff and making nasty comments about our garden."

Mom's considering, like she wants to believe them. But then she says, "I just can't get beyond the fact that you took the guns without permission, and you threatened to kill Bentley, and now she's dead!"

"We didn't do it!" Johnny exclaims and then repeats. "We didn't do it!" He seems like he could actually blubber.

Mom gives this huge sigh. "I'd like to believe you, boys." Her voice has a dead sound. "But it's too much for me to automatically believe you didn't do it when you made the threat. Maybe you wish you hadn't, but regret won't bring her back. It's something we're all going to have to live with. When something like this is done, there's no going back!"

Mike grabs Johnny and yanks him out of the room. "I knew she wouldn't listen. I told you it wouldn't do any good."

"Bentley had two bullet holes through her!" Mom exclaims after them. "I'm sorry, but how could I get beyond that!"

They rush out the kitchen and bump my stool over on the way. As I pick myself up I imagine I'm jabbing them with lots of little pins, like they are voodoo dolls.

Much later at night, long after I'm supposed to be in bed asleep, I'm sitting beside my window looking out to the garden at the ugly brown patch of earth. At first I think of Bentley deep in the earth, surrounded and trapped, but it's too horrible. So then I think maybe she could become like a ghost and escape.

She could be thin, like a gas or a mist, and rise up through the earth. If she did that I could see her again. She'd be there in the moonlight, misty and light, but in her same form, and she'd pounce and roll and stretch, with her brilliant eyes staring at me. All the rest of her would be misty, but not her eyes. They would be real. Then I would know that her spirit, at least, was not gone.

With overpowering yearning, I strain my eyes into the moonlight to look for her. It's a long time, but no matter how hard I look and pray and imagine, nothing is there.

I'm sitting at the window and have gone just a little bit asleep when I'm suddenly awakened by the sound of loud, angry voices. It's Mom and Dad. Dad must have just come back from Uncle Canute's. They're arguing, shouting. From Mom, furious, "I don't care!"

Most of Dad's answer I can't hear. "—Canute. I may as well—if I can't—something I enjoy!"

I'm very tired and I'm desperate for sleep. It's all like a nightmare, but when I glance around I see Mike and Johnny moving like shadows out in the hallway. They're creeping along on their hands and feet past the doorway of my room. If they go on their hands and feet, the floor doesn't squeak.

I get down on my hands and feet and start out of my room behind them. As soon as Mike notices me he nudges Johnny, and they both motion and silently mouth to me, "Get!" I respond with my most fierce glare.

"If we can't get this settled," Dad's shouting, "if I can't have anything that I want, something I treasure—!"

"Like Halley treasured Bentley!" Mom interrupts. "Bentley was killed with your precious treasures! Don't tell me about treasures! You had no right to bring those guns here. Bentley's dead, and a child's heart is broken because of your selfishness and stupidity!"

"I'm not entirely sure the boys did that," Dad declares. "If they did, it was probably an accident."

"Oh, so you think, probably! You're not sure!" Mom exclaims.

"I knew it was a mistake to come back!" Dad practically shouts. "Don't think I'll make that mistake again! Just as soon as I can make some other arrangement, I will!"

Johnny and Mike exchange meaningful glances. I notice Johnny shudder.

I feel like the floor is about to collapse under me and I will fall into an abyss. Suddenly I'm up and screaming and kicking them. "It's all your fault, you killers! You ruined everything!" I'm pounding and kicking them with my bare feet.

Mike jumps up, grabs me, and pins my arms. Johnny wraps himself around my feet. Dad bounds to the bottom of the stairs. "You kids get to bed, now! If I hear another word from any of you, you'll be sorry!"

Mike turns me loose with a tremendous shove that sends me to the floor on my face. I bound to my feet and shake my fist at him. He goes to shove me again, but I duck to one side and Johnny gets it instead, hitting the wall hard. He comes back at Mike, punching him and calling him a rotten, stupid crap head.

Dad's coming up the stairs. With my hands over my ears I fly into my room, jump into bed, and cover my head with my pillow. Dad rushes past my room to the boys and stands at their door making threats.

After a while he leaves, and then everything in their room and downstairs gets quiet. I try to sleep. I really try, but it's like there are a thousand voices inside of me, and all of them are accusing each other. I'm lying flat on my bed, trying to be calm, but the voices won't stop. I turn one way and then another. I even try putting my face on the bed and my butt in the air. Nothing works.

Always before, I went to sleep with Bentley in my arms. She was like a stuffed animal, except that because she was real, she was so much better. Even on the hottest summer nights, when I couldn't actually stand her touching my body because she made me hot, I put her on my face and just lifted her off now and then to breathe.

She was so soft and fluffy, and she purred so loud she

sounded like a pot boiling on the stove. She'd scrape her rough tongue over my ear, and her big, fluffy tail would slowly float back and forth like a fan while she kneaded my shoulder with her paws.

Oh, Bentley, Bentley! So much is lost! You! Everything! My arms ache to hold you, and there's no way I can get settled. Edgar says hating makes you sick! But sometimes it's the only thing that helps!

The house is quiet, and I can hear the big clock ticking in the foyer. I'm quiet on the outside, but the thousands of thoughts are bumping into each other in my mind. They're racing around and having accidents in my brain.

Slowly I slip out of bed. Taking one careful step at a time, I cross my room to the hall. Then I start down the stairs, waiting after each step before I take the next one until I'm all the way to the bottom.

There I stand for a while. It seems like I'm asleep, but then I awaken and move slowly through the kitchen and into the laundry room.

When I get there I just stand looking at everything. One of Mike's T-shirts is on the washer, Mom's sewing box is on the counter. Slowly I reach into it and ease out her scissors. Then, holding the shirt with one hand and the scissors in the other, I make a very tiny cut in the shirt.

It's in the hem. I cut a little more, about an inch. Now the shirt is changed. I cut more. With long, purposeful motions I cut and cut until the shirt is open from the bottom to the neck. Then I just stand there and stare at it.

It looks sort of like a jacket, and it's somehow—better, freer. I think it's almost—improved.

But it's still one piece, still a shirt. Next, I cut a strip. Now there's a part of it that's completely free of the rest. I cut more and more until the whole shirt is in strips.

Then, cutting rapidly, I start on a pair of jeans. When they are in long strips I go to another pair. Then socks, and undershorts, more shirts and shorts. All of them Mike's and Johnny's clothes. I'm standing and cutting for a long time.

I cut until I can't find any more of their clothes, and then I stand looking around. There are piles of strips all over the laundry room. I go about the room and gather them into one humongous pile. When I put my arms around it, it's so big I can barely see over it.

Carefully I make my way out of the laundry and across the family room, putting the pile down to unlock the door to the patio and then picking it up again and going outside. At the edge of the patio I feel down carefully with my toe until I touch the grass. It is cold and wet from the dew, and as I step down the sudden coldness and wetness on my feet sends little waves of shock through me.

I cross the yard with my burden and drop it on Bentley's grave. Then I lean over and spread it around until all of the ugly brown earth is covered. Stepping back in the silver moonlight I survey the mound, which is now dressed in a riotous heap of color, a mountain of ribbonlike strips.

Some of the strips have fallen, and I follow their trail back to the house. Now I can go to bed. Now I can sleep.

16

I'm awakened by a loud yell, "What! What the . . . !" At first I don't remember, and I think some terrible thing has happened, like maybe a wild animal with rabies has gotten into the kitchen.

Mike and Johnny speed past my bedroom doorway, Dad starts exclaiming, and then I remember.

Mom starts with, "What!" and goes to, "Who!"

Under my quilt I'm warm and comfortable. I thought I'd never feel safe and comfortable in bed again, not without Bentley. Soon they'll come and scream at me, and I'll have to take my punishment. I shudder when I think how awful it'll be. There are doors slamming and more exclaiming.

I'll just wait and not even try to escape. Or maybe I'll go down so they can start on me right away. I'll stand, and their rage will hit me like an atomic blast.

A long while goes by and nothing happens. I get up, go to the bathroom, and then back to my room to dress. Downstairs all the exclaiming has stopped, and there is just quiet murmuring. It's so quiet, I can't hear anything. It's quieter than it has ever been.

I'm completely dressed and sitting on my bed. Out the window I can see Bentley's grave, colorful, with white from the underwear gleaming in the early morning light and accenting the colored strips. It won't stay there, I know. They'll bring it in or make me bring it in.

Mom and Mike and Johnny come up the stairs, and I think, now! They're coming! They're going to punish me severely. But they just pass my room without even looking in. I hear the attic pull-down stairs squeak and then them going up.

From the attic I hear Mom. "This'll have to do until we get more." There are exclamations and groans and then laughs. "Use a belt and gather them up," she says. "Like that. Yes."

"You'll lose them!" Mike is exclaiming.

"Yours have paint stains," Johnny says, "and a big hole there."

"That's what they were, paint rags," Mom says. Her voice is very calm.

They don't say anything when they come down. They just go back past my room and down the stairs.

After they're down, I get my homework. Maybe I'll be able to escape. I'll dash out and get on the school bus. The TV's on. Above it I hear Mike. All I can catch is, ". . . guys . . . think we look stupid."

Then I hear Mom, but I can't make out any of her words.

Dad calls from the other room, something like, "That's just the way it is."

It's time for the bus. I start down the stairs quietly. With each step I expect to be attacked by one or two or all four of them. Step, nothing. Step, very quiet step.

More steps. Nothing. On, until I'm down. Then I grab the door handle and dash out.

No one is behind me. No one calls, threatens, or demands that I come back.

The bus is lumbering up the hill and around the bend, and Mike and Johnny speed past me and jump on as soon as it stops. Since the schools are so close, elementary and junior high, we all go on the same bus together.

I step on and immediately hear the kids laughing. Gary Sower jeers at them, "Look at them dumb hillbillies!" His mother is the one who always stands in her backyard and swears at us.

His brother, Eddie, calls, "Hicks, look at the stupid hicks."

There are others saying things and laughing. I hear from Mike, "Ask Halley. She did it. She's the one who's nuts."

All day I get questions, but I just respond with a shrug or a "So what!"

I keep thinking, after school my whole family will get me. They didn't yet because they have to think all day to come up with something really awful to do to me, but when I walk in I'll really get it!

After school when I actually walk in, Mom glances at me and says, "Hurry and change, Halley. We're leaving in five minutes."

I haven't actually looked at any member of my family since the night before, which seems like years away.

I change and then go down to the family room where Mom's rearranging boxes from an auction. She comes toward me, and I'm looking at the floor thinking, now! In a second I'll be flat, squashed like a bug. But it doesn't happen. Instead she just picks up a heavy box and shoves it at me. "Here, take this. Carry that with one hand, and put this knapsack full of doilies on your shoulder. That'll leave your other hand free for these. Now, they're heavy, don't drop them."

She picks up a lot of other things and starts out the door. We're going to walk. The whole way I'm thinking, she's going to yell or scream or cry. She's going to do something. The very least is that she'll tell me I have to wear rags, too. Or maybe she's thinking of locking me in the back of her stand for a year, or never letting me leave her side, just chaining me with an iron band around my wrist and making me sleep on a mat on the floor beside her bed, chained to the bed leg, so I can never sneak around in the night again.

Or, she's going to tell me she's giving me to a traveling circus for their freak show. They'll put me in a cage with a sign, THE CUTTING KID.

The most likely thing she's planning is to hit me with the large paddle she has for sale at her stand. The reason we're going there is she has to go get it. Of all the things I'm thinking, that's the one that'll hurt the least.

She doesn't look at me at all, except for quick glances when she doesn't think I'll notice. She looks worried. The most I can hope for, I decide, is a week of really loud, critical talk and then it just getting less and less, slowly, so it's over maybe by Christmas.

We get to her stand and she tells me where to put the stuff I'm carrying. I do it ultra carefully, but when I'm finished, she just ignores me.

I just stand and wait. Kirk has seen us, and he's coming. When he gets there I say, aiming my words in her
general direction, "Guess I'll go with Kirk now."

I expect her to explode, "Not a chance! Don't move
an inch!" But she just looks at me with her new "you're
a stranger" look and then goes back to her inventory.

Kirk notices the look. As I ease away with him, he
glances back, and then when we're pretty far away he
says, "You're in trouble." When I don't answer, he just
lets it drop. "What do you want to do?"

Usually I'm the one who suggests things to do, and
he's the one who agrees. I just shrug. He gives me a
sharp look. Kirk can read the wind. "We could fish."
He's looking at me to see what I think. But I don't care.

"We could gather all kinds of leaves. Edgar knows
how to preserve them in epoxy so they stay the same.
But you have to press them first. Then the epoxy hard-
ens, and they stay the same forever."

I sigh. "I did that last fall. But, okay, that's fun."

"If you want to do something else . . ."

"No."

"We can't get really good ones here. We'll have to go
to the woods."

I look back at Mom's stand. She has a customer, but
she can see me plainly and she's not motioning me back
or anything.

The woods are a golden haze beyond the two big
fields, and we set out for them. When we get up there,
I turn and look out to the distance. "There's Dinky's
Bluff. Mom took me there. She cried and cried."

Kirk glances at me quickly and then away. He's

embarrassed. Quietly, almost shyly, he asks, "Why?"

"Because everything's so crummy."

"Your dad, and her, and like that?"

"Yeah."

He grunts, "Mmm." Then he starts going from tree to tree getting leaves. With each leaf he says the name, and when he has a bunch he hands them to me to sort. He's admiring a huge barrel of a tree, and says, "Beeches are my favorite."

I've never heard him talk so much, and I don't really care. But after a while I ask, "How can you tell what's what? I don't know one from the other."

"Edgar," he says. "He knows them all."

I say to him, "Edgar knows a lot."

"Yeah," Kirk agrees. "I wish I knew his mother."

I just look at him. "Edgar? His mother?" I don't say it, but it seems odd to even think of Edgar having a mother. "That would be your . . . great . . . something."

"Yeah. She thought Edgar was beautiful."

"Was she blind?"

Kirk looks at me funny and then grins.

I'm immediately terribly embarrassed. "I didn't mean—I mean, I know he's deformed—"

Kirk laughs. "I said that to him. He told me she wasn't blind. She just thought that because, before he was born when he was inside of her, her husband—that was Edgar's father—kicked her, and it made this water come out that babies float in. So she thought Edgar was dead inside of her. The powwow doctor and everyone told her that her baby—that was Edgar—was dead. They said she was like a tomb carrying around a dead baby.

"But then when she had him and he was alive, she thought he was beautiful. She said his eyes were beautiful and his head was beautiful, and his nose and ears and mouth were all beautiful. . . ."

"She didn't notice that he didn't have any arms or legs or feet?"

"I guess she noticed, but she expected him to be dead, so when he wasn't, she thought he was at least better than that. Everyone on the reservation thou—"

"Reservation!"

"Yeah, Edgar's a Seneca . . ."

"A Seneca? You mean like an Indian? Like from a tribe?"

Kirk nods. "Half. His father was an Indian, but his mother wasn't."

I'm really excited. "Then you're an Indian! If he's an Indian, then you're one, too! Sort of. He's your real grandfather, isn't he?"

He nods.

I'm looking at him like he has become this whole different person.

"Edgar said if his mother knew me, she'd think I was clever and capable. She thought he was clever and capable."

We have a huge pile of leaves and we're sitting at the edge of the woods sorting them. I'm leaning against a tree trunk looking down across the fields to the town. Mike and Johnny are playing hockey around the firehouse with three other boys.

I just kind of announce to the air, "Mike and Johnny had on ratty clothes today."

"Because you cut up their other clothes?"

"Who told you?"

"Eddie Sower. Did you?" He has a stick and he's sitting, tapping his shoe with it.

I don't answer, and I know if I wait long enough he'll just start talking about something else. "They killed Bentley." He doesn't say anything. "And they lied and said they didn't. I could tell Mom I saw them cutting up their own clothes. I could say I was thirsty and went down to the refrigerator to get a drink and saw them in there doing it."

Kirk looks away and stops hitting his foot. "But you'd just be doing that to get them in trouble instead of you, right?"

"Yeah, but doesn't anybody care about Bentley! They're not being punished for killing her!"

Kirk stands up. "We have to get the leaves pressed or they'll dry out and curl up." He's looking out to the distance where the sky and the land come together. We start for the Dragon. All the time he doesn't say anything, but he has this look.

Finally I just stop, turn around to look at him, and demand, "What?"

"Nothing."

"You think I'm horrible to even imagine telling a lie to get Mike and Johnny in trouble, don't you?"

His big gray eyes settle upon me. "Would you swear to God that you saw them do it?"

"They swore to God that they didn't kill Bentley."
We're at the fence. It's just an electric wire, and I drop
down and roll under it. Kirk goes way back to get a
good run so he can jump over it.

"You're going to get shock-butt if you miss," I call to
him.

He runs, jumps, and sails over it easily. Then he tells
me, "The electricity isn't on."

"How do you know?"

"No one would waste electricity to fence in corn."

I say to him, laughing, "Unless they have restless
corn."

We're halfway up the street, and I stop walking. He
turns around to see why I'm not coming. "You know I'd
never actually say they did it," I tell him. "I was just
thinking."

He turns around and starts walking again, his troubled expression easing.

"Still, I'm going to get it, no matter what! I'll probably
get killed once Mom thinks about it some more. Or
Dad. Pray for me."

"I always do," he says.

17

I have to go to counseling three times a week. My counselor is a doofus.

Dad didn't go to Uncle Canute's like he threatened, but he and Mom haven't been talking to each other for a long while, except about things like, why is the water heater leaking?

It's noon on a Saturday in October, and Mom and I are coming up the hill from the Dragon. We were there all morning, but Dad and the boys weren't. They never come to the Dragon anymore.

Mom has hired someone to work her stand, and she's trying to spend a lot more time with me. Like, we're going to an auction after lunch. I got off easy. Even Kirk says so, and I'm not going to do or say anything for a long time. I'll be as bland as mashed potatoes.

Dad's mowing, and the boys are raking leaves. Mom fills three watering cans and tells me to do the hanging baskets on the porch. All of a sudden there's a loud roar, and we all whip around. A car, a gorgeous red convertible, eases up to our front gate like a large red cat, and the roaring stops.

A beautiful woman opens the door and steps out. Her motions seem fluid. She moves like even the simplest thing, like getting out of the car, is ballet, and I know immediately who she is, she's Boots. Not that I recognize her from her picture or remember her from the last time. I just know.

Mike is gripping his rake like it's a cane that he needs to use to keep from falling over. Johnny has dropped his rake and he's just standing there with his mouth open, looking stupid.

They only stare for a moment, and then they both run to her and she sweeps them into her arms. She's exclaiming and kissing, hugging and laughing. Dad forces himself to continue mowing, but when I glance at him I can see the muscles in his jaw clamping hard.

Mom's watching. With her limp hair and her jeans and flannel shirt, I think right away what a contrast she is to the beautiful woman.

Boots has on a short, silver leather jumper, which gleams in the golden, autumn sun. Her hair is dark and curly, and it's pulled high on her head with a few stray long curls that sweep across her face as she moves. Her nails are very long and brilliant red.

She doesn't look like the woman in the torn-up puzzle picture that Kirk has, but she is. In the picture she was actually prettier, soft and glowing. Now she's dramatic and beautiful.

I'm swinging around the light post, and with every swing I look at her and imprint the look on my brain before I swing around again for another look. Her voice is like water music. "Canute called and said my boys needed me."

I glance at Dad. His jaw looks permanently clamped.

Mom's just plain glaring. Dad has been trying to ignore Boots, but he fails, and shuts off the mower engine.

Boots comes up the walk with her arms around Mike's and Johnny's shoulders. They're not looking at her or each other or Mom and Dad or me. It's like they're seeing stars or some distant thing that no one else can see.

She takes a quick, sweeping look at the house, the yard, everywhere, and then she says, "So." Excitement and warmth seem to radiate from her like a vapor. They linger in the air around her. She's magnetic. Just standing near her I feel like she is sunshine, and she could be my best and most special friend forever.

Mom's scowling, and Dad's frowning. I want to jump between them and her, to protect her from them. I want to say, "Don't notice. They don't mean it."

Mike and Johnny look like they have been transformed into mush.

Mom's the first to say something. "So, you came back." Her tone is bitter and harsh. I feel as though the words will cut Boots, and if she is cut I will bleed. "Your sons looked for you for years, but they finally stopped, and now you're here."

Boots's gaze at Mom is warm and gracious, like she can understand and forgive any malice, no matter how great. "Yes," she says softly, "now I'm here."

She turns to Dad. "They'll come with me?" It's a gentle, almost shy question hinged just upon him.

He looks like he's exploding inside, but he nods.

Suddenly I'm thinking, what is this? Go away! No, they can't! It's not supposed to be this way! Then I have to fight down the most ridiculous, off base thought I've ever had, which is, if you take them, take me, too. She isn't even my mother. But the radiance, the life that's a part of her, that just sweeps out from her, is swirling around and through me.

In an excited voice she's telling them to get their clothes, but then she seems to see their rags for the first time. They got new clothes for church and school, but they still have to wear the old, horrible clothes when we're working outside. Boots throws a momentarily accusing look at Mom and Dad and then says, "Oh, never mind. I'll get you some new ones."

The boys look at Dad and then Mom. They definitely don't look at me.

"Okay," Dad says reluctantly. "I guess it's . . . they're in school, you know, Boots. They'll have to make up what they miss. How long . . . ?"

Boots waves her hand like she's waving away a little cloud that has floated in front of her. "Oh, we'll just see."

Mike and Johnny are still not looking at anything, not her or Mom or Dad. Now more than ever I miss Bentley. She'd be wrapped around my neck like a scarf, and my hands would be upon her, constantly stroking.

Mike's already at the car, and Johnny's right behind him. It's like they want to make sure they're stationed in her space in case something comes up that might prevent them from going.

Dad steps forward and raises his hand, like he's about to get them, but then he lets it fall and steps back. It's imaginary, his space and her space, but some things that are imaginary are also real. He sends his voice to them in her space where he won't go. "Don't forget, sons."

Mike and Johnny both nod.

I don't know what they're not supposed to forget. Him? Us? Everything? They climb into the car, Johnny in front and Mike in the back.

I look at the letters on the side and pronounce, "Ma-se-ra-ti."

Mike pronounces it quickly, looking at me like I'm a worm, "Maserati," and then looks away.

I say, not to him, just to myself, "I never heard of that." It's like Boots is seeing me for the first time, just me. She glances from me to Dad and back to me.

"So this is your girl, Tim." Her eyes beam upon me like warm velvet, and I am enveloped in a smile that says we, just she and I, are alone and are sharing a wonderful, great, private joy.

For a moment I have to fight down the thought, why couldn't she be my mother? It's a traitor thought, and I squash it down instantly.

Suddenly I wish Kirk were here and could meet her. He has no mother at all. He'd really wish he had one like her.

The red Maserati roars away, and Mike and Johnny don't even wave good-bye. That's the worst part. Brothers shouldn't just happily roar out of your life without a backward glance.

After they leave, Dad mumbles something about having to go into the office for a while, and he gets in the car and leaves, too. Then Mom sits down and cries.

"Are we going to the Dragon?" I ask. I want to get her mind off crying.

She just shakes her head. "Go, if you want to. Just go. Everyone's leaving, you might as well, too."

"No, I think I'll stay here," I tell her.

"Go," she says. "I'm going to talk on the phone. You don't need to stay here. You don't need the stress. You've had too much already. That's what's wrong with you. Go play."

I look at her for a moment. She's serious. She really wants me to go. I skip down the path. All the way down by the creek I'm thinking, that's what's wrong with me? Stress? Is there anything wrong with me? If my counselor weren't such a doofus I'd ask him if he really thought there was something wrong with me. But he is a doofus, so I won't.

When I see Kirk I say to him, "My brothers went away. My dream came true." I just walk past him on the way to my picture.

The Dragon is open and full. I want to go where I don't have to look at anyone, inside where it's cool and dark. When Kirk comes in, I just say to him over and over, "I didn't mean it to be like this."

18

After three days the phone rings and I answer. It's Johnny. "Hello, Halley? Is Mom there?"

"No." In the background I hear the deep bark of a big dog. "Whose dog is that?"

He's speaking to someone else with his voice muffled. Then he asks, "Is Dad there?"

"He's in the garage. I'll get him."

Dad comes and takes the phone, and all I hear is, "Uh-huh, uh-huh." I go into his study and pick up the other phone.

Both Mike and Johnny are talking, telling Dad about a huge pool and a Jacuzzi. I don't say anything, because if I did all three of them would immediately tell me to hang up. They start describing a multilevel trampoline that I can't even imagine, and then they say there are three rottweilers where they are, and it's a huge, stone house.

All of it sounds really great. It's supposed to, but I wonder if Dad can hear in their voices that it's not.

"Who's there with you?" Dad asks.

"Mommy and Henry Martin." The voices sound lost. "It's his place."

"What's he like?" Dad asks. "Is he okay?"

There are hollow-sounding "Yeah"s.

"Put Boots on."

There's muffled talk, and then her voice, warm and soothing. "Yes, Tim?"

"Names and addresses, Boots," Dad snaps. "And you know this can't last."

"Of course not, Tim," she murmurs. "Nothing can. But they are my sons, and this is my time. You've had them, and they tell me things weren't going well—their clothes destroyed? And they're accused of killing their sister's cat? Tim, really! They didn't, they wouldn't—"

Dad's furious. "None of this is any of your business! I can't believe Canute sicced you on us! Traitors come in all disguises!"

I hear Mike and Johnny exclaiming behind covered receivers, and Boots is speaking soothingly. Then she says, "He didn't sic me on you, Tim. Canute and I talk. He's been my lifeline when I was so low, I didn't think I could go on . . ." Her voice trails off.

I feel like putting my hand out to her through the long distance over the phone, putting my arm around her and bearing her up.

"I'll give you two weeks to play Mommy," Dad says. "And then you get them back here. They'll have a hard enough time making up the difference in school as it is."

The soft voice says, "So angry, Tim. Did I hurt you so much? Do I deserve so little?"

Dad says with just a little less anger, "You can't do this."

"I know," she says. "I know."

* * *

Dad and Mom talk a lot about the situation, but not to each other. They talk on the phone for hours to other people. I overhear Mom saying to her best friend, Lauren, "It's a problem, and Tim and I should be working together to solve it, but he won't. I just have to accept that."

Dad's talking to Canute. "Yeah, well. It's no use here. That's just the way it is. I don't know what's down the road." I listen a lot, because the house is so quiet with Mike and Johnny gone, there's nothing else to hear.

I think there has to be something I can do.

Mom talks most of the time to Lauren, but she also talks to someone named David. One day Lauren is there. I hear Mom and Lauren talking about him, and Lauren says, "He never got over you, Gwen."

Mom sighs. "Well, I've known David for a long time. There never was a kinder, gentler man than David."

They make me sick. I can just see Mom going off with marvelous David. And me? Where does that leave me? Nowhere, is my guess. Or living with Dad sometimes, and Mom and David the rest of the time and belonging nowhere.

It's early November with beautiful, hazy days and the smell of dust and smoke, but I can't think about anything. Mike and Johnny have been gone for two weeks, and Dad's talking to a lawyer about getting them back.

On a Saturday afternoon I'm at home alone with him. He's cleaning the mower blades, and he looks up when I walk by with my paddleball set. "You'd like it in

Lakeport where Canute lives, Halley. There's the lake
and . . ."

My teeth nearly fall out. He's thinking of moving and
taking me with him? Without Mom! Is he nuts? My
answer is absolute silence, and I turn away. I don't even
look at him. He goes on for a while about the lake, but
since it's a strictly one-way conversation, he soon gives
up.

Lucky for him, lucky for me, because I've been hardly
able to restrain myself from running over to him and
kicking his shins and pounding on his face with my fists
and shouting in his face that mothers aren't for leaving.
But then neither are fathers. It's the sort of thing that
puts a big, ugly scar right down the middle of a kid.
Not a scar anyone can see, but it feels real. The kid
knows it's there.

A few days after that, Mom and I are at the Dragon,
going from stand to stand to get fruits and fresh vegetables. I'm trying to get her to stop for sundaes when
a tall man suddenly appears in front of us and the name
"David!" comes from Mom. The way she says it is
sharp, surprised, and full of meaning.

He's handsome, like her friend said, and he has a kind
face. Right away I know I have to be against him. Dad
isn't particularly tall or handsome.

"Gwen," David says. Each of them says the other's
name like it's a whole week's conversation. I jiggle
Mom's arm to be distractive, and she says, "David, this
is my daughter. You never met her."

David looks at me with a pleasant, open expression,

but he quickly sucks in his breath when he sees the hostility I have in my eyes. He reads it instantly. David, I can see, is no dummy. Anything he has intended to say to me escapes him.

Mom begins talking to him about her friend, Lauren, and then she goes on to ask about his mother. They are talking about other people they both know, people I've never heard of, or only heard of once or twice.

David has on trousers that have cuffs. The cuffs are like little, all-around pockets. His shoes are shined, and Mom's and his eyes are on each other above my head. The side of the street is dirt, packed hard, but with all the people walking over it, bits of dirt have come loose.

I begin to kick the dirt, not thinking at first, but every time I kick, a little spray of dust flies up and settles on David's shiny shoes. When I see that, I give another small kick.

He glances down when a tiny pebble hits his shoe. Mom doesn't notice. She's talking. He looks at me to see if I've noticed that I'm kicking dirt on him, and as soon as he does he receives another look of crystallized malice. Mom asks him a question, and he looks up to answer her.

I begin kicking dirt in earnest, then. Not with much force or Mom'll notice, but very rhythmically. There isn't a lot each time, but hundreds of tiny sprays of dust will eventually fill anything. With each kick David's trouser cuffs and shoes are slowly filling.

He shoots me a pointed glance and then moves to Mom's other side to continue the conversation.

I don't follow him immediately. That would be too

obvious. But slowly I begin to work my way around. Mom isn't aware of me at all. I could be on another planet as far as she's concerned. She's in a different world with people I don't even know. She's talking like a different person, and she sounds young and fresh, excited and full of hope.

David's eyes glow when he looks at her. He can hardly drag his eyes from her. But every so often he has to, because with each seemingly aimless motion I'm getting closer to him again, maneuvering into dirt-kicking range. And whenever he glances at me he can see the menace that I intend to be to him because of the menace that I think he is to me.

I can see that he wants to laugh. He wants to say, "Hey, kid, I see what you're doing. Nice try." After a while I almost have to laugh, too. Because his whole cuff is sagging with dust, and his shoes where they gape at the sides are filled with it. He doesn't say anything.

Dad will never know what I'm doing for him, for us, I think, as David and Mom begin a reluctant good-bye.

As she turns to go, Mom exclaims, "Oh, Halley, look what you've done! Just look! You've been standing there kicking dirt like a fool! You've gotten dust all over David! Oh, girl, what am I going to do with you!" To David she says, her voice dripping with apology, "I'm so sorry. She just never does think."

David brushes his trousers and shoes several times. He says, "Don't worry about it, Gwen. It's all right." He gives me a hard look.

19

It's afternoon, and I'm on the way home from school. The bus is laboring up the hill toward our house. When it rounds the curve, I look out and see a silver-colored convertible in front of our house. The top is down, and there are three big rottweilers in the backseat. Mike and Johnny are home.

Boots is there with a man who, the minute I walk in, says to me, "So, this is Halley!" He gives me an exaggerated wink as he comes toward me with his hand out. "Well, well! So, this is THE Halley. I'm Henry Martin, but since you're THE Halley, you can call me Enrico Martino."

Boots thinks that's funny. She starts laughing, and she keeps on laughing until she's nearly crying. I'm trying to figure out what's so funny.

Henry/Enrico has on a suit that's made of smooth, silky, gray material. His shirt is gleaming white, and he's wearing cuff links. I can't take my eyes off the cuff links. There is something about him that makes him seem desperate, and he makes me feel shy. I don't know why, but before I look at him very long I feel sorry for him, and I feel sorry for Boots because she's with him.

When he looks at Boots he seems dazed, but it's like

he's almost afraid of her, too. When she looks at him she laughs too much.

By the time I arrive they've already started saying good-bye. Boots says to the boys, "Well, back to the grind, boys, school and all." It seems, when she looks at each of them, she's trying to get every detail of them and press it into her mind. I'm thinking, how can they let each other go?

Mike and Johnny look upset, and I'm wondering why. Are they disappointed because she has to go? Or didn't they like being with her? I would.

Her voice is low and tender. "I'll come for you this summer, right?"

Mike manages, "Yeah, sure," but it sounds like he doesn't believe her. She looks at him like he has driven a pike through her heart. I want to reach out personally and shelter her from the pain.

"I'll come this summer, Michael, I will! No more time lost between us, no more lost years. I promise. We're together now." Her fingers are crossed to show how together they are, but it occurs to me that crossing your fingers can also mean you're lying. Mike is focusing on the crossed fingers, and I know he's thinking that, too.

Johnny's hanging back and not looking at her. I'm thinking, I can't feel sorry for him. He murdered Bentley, I can't ever feel sorry for someone who did that. I have to remember and make myself never care about either of them, no matter what.

Mike's nodding. In three weeks he has grown bigger.

I wonder, have I? It's odd to be changing all the time, with grown-ups just staying the same.

The man—I'm thinking of him as Henrico—says as they turn to go, "It's been a blast, guys. See ya." When I look at him, it comes to me that he's someone who spends all of his time trying to be someone else.

The boys go into the house and they don't even wave when Boots leaves. Mom and Dad just give her good-byes, accompanied by unfriendly glares. I'm the one who says good-bye to her with friendship and caring. She looks at me surprised, and then bends down and gives me a kiss. "Good-bye, Halley," she says. "Be good to my boys."

Be good to her boys! Is she kidding? She could tell them to be good to me, but then I forgive her instant-ly. She doesn't know what monsters they are. She could never imagine them doing something like killing Bentley. Not her. It's right that she thinks they're won-derful. A real mother should.

After she leaves I go into the house. Mike and Johnny are out on the patio, alone. I go out to the patio, too, and flop onto the hammock. I'm not going to say anything. It gets me in trouble. One thing I'd like to say is, "Bet you never thought of shooting their rottweilers."

It's odd having them back. Whenever the feeling comes that it's good they're back, I pound it into a men-tal picture of Bentley at the moment of death. Then I don't have any trouble, it's easy hating them again.

I can't understand why I have to remind myself to be

angry to keep from being glad they're back. My counselor would love to chew on that one. He'd think he was
earning his salary if he could get me to sort through my
emotions and put them in nice, neat little categories. But
I'm not going to give him the satisfaction.

I'm not going to spend any energy on how much I
don't like him. It's just like, if everybody and everything
were a restaurant meal that I didn't like, he'd be pickles
on the side. The main part would be Mike and Johnny,
with David being another whole serving, and even
Mom and Dad being, maybe, a salad. Of course, liking
and not liking someone can change really fast. I didn't
think I liked Boots, but it only took one second for me
to find out that I did.

My counselor would come up with a lot of comments
on that. He's a Christian counselor, so he's really for
positive thinking. He's always quoting the Bible on hate
and vengeance. I'd like to find "doofus" in the Bible and
say, "Here, read this one. It's about you."

He's so hung up on clothes cutting! And even Kirk
understands that cutting up their clothes was like cutting up their skin, only doing it so it didn't really hurt.
It was like telling them, "I should cut up your skin for
what you did, but I wouldn't."

As soon as they're home for about four hours, Mike
and Johnny can see what a mess the family is in. Their
first clue is Mom on the phone to David. Johnny asks
me in a whisper, "Who's David?"

"A jerk," I tell him. "He works in town, but he's taking
over the place down at the Dragon that used to sell ice

cream, just opening on evenings and weekends. Mom talks to him all the time. She's a jerk, too."

Johnny's eyes are very wide.

"Dad and Mom are both jerks," I tell them.

Mike surprises me. "I don't think Mom's a jerk."

So, I tell him about David, and when I get to the part about the cuffs, both of them say, "Way to go, Hal! Good job!"

Then Mike says, "Show me this guy."

"I thought you wanted them to get divorced."

They both look at me like I'm off my rocker. Johnny says, "No! I don't want that. That would be terrible!"

"Why would you think we'd want that?" Mike asks.

"Well, if they did, you could just go and live with Boots. That's what you want, isn't it? To go and live with her? And maybe you could even persuade her and Dad to get married again, if she isn't already married to Henrico. She isn't, is she?" They're just looking at me.

"What I can't figure is why she came for you now when she didn't before."

Johnny's looking at the ceiling. "Uncle Canute," he says.

"You mean Uncle Canute called her and told her to come and see you?"

"Something like that," from Mike.

"Oh." I'm quiet for a while, thinking, but then I have to ask, "Did you like her? I mean, was she . . . ?" It feels really stupid asking if they liked their mother. "I did. I liked her."

Johnny breathes softly, "Yeah."

"But why didn't she come before?" I ask, and then I just decide to shut up.

"She's okay," Mike says. "It's complicated." They both look grim and almost angry. "It's just, we'd never want to live with her," he adds.

I feel shy talking about it, but I offer, "I really liked her." They both look at me, and Johnny nods slowly.

Mike says, "Still, it's best if she just visits."

"Henrico has an Olympic-size swimming pool," Johnny says. "And a three-level trampoline."

"I heard that. I was listening the night you called Dad."

"That stuff was great. He has this huge place, and a gardener and a maid."

"Did they want you to stay?"

Mike answers carefully, "They said they did . . ."

Johnny adds in a wistful tone, "But it wouldn't work out."

"No," Mike agrees.

Later I'm talking to Kirk, and I say to him, "I thought they wanted our family to wreck, but now they don't." I'm telling him about the three rottweilers and Henrico and that they liked my dust-kicking job on David.

David is fixing up his stand. Some of the Dragon's stands have nice grass and flowers around them, like Mom's. But others have just weeds or whatever and paint that's peeling off. David's stand was old and ugly, but he's putting ruffled wood all around it to make it look old-fashioned. And he's painting it two different colors of pink and two different colors of green, with bright gold lettering. It looks really fabulous. He's going to sell jellies and herbs.

Mom's always talking to him and admiring what he's doing. Outside of his stand are two carousel horses that he carved and painted himself. His stand's going to be the best-looking one in the whole Dragon. Mom tells him she loves his instinct for creativity.

I tell Mike and Johnny we have to get rid of David, and after we talk about it for a while we come up with a plan. We'll always, one of us, be at his stand when there are people around, and we'll have comments, like that we found mouse droppings in his jellies. Or we'll mention that his herbs were grown where they spray lots of poisonous chemicals. We come up with a plan to buy a jar of his jelly and then stand around and look disgusted as we pretend to pull hairs out of it.

Mike and Johnny and Kirk and I are in Edgar's warehouse, sitting on the two leather club chairs and matching leather sofa, discussing our plan to get rid of David. Mike's holding a jar of fuzzy mold and telling us that we can say it came from David's jelly. "There has to be someone on duty at his stand all the time," Mike says. "We have to stick together on this, or we'll never get rid of him."

Mike and Johnny get up to leave, and Kirk whispers to me, "I'm going to give them their picture, all right? I don't know what else to do with it."

I look at him, and at first I'm thinking, no way. But then I say, "Okay, if you want to, I don't care."

"Hey, Mike, Johnny," he calls, and when they come back Kirk looks kind of shy. He always looks shy around them, but he says, "I have something that's yours. You probably don't want it, but you can throw it away or whatever." He goes over to the door that leads into his and Edgar's living area. I don't follow them. I stay in front of my ocean picture.

After a while Kirk comes back and flops down beside me. "They took it."

"They didn't even say thank you, did they?"

"No, but that's okay."

20

Pastor Linkous shows up at our door on a Monday night. He not only preaches in our church but he's our school janitor. Mike and Johnny and I are immediately at the top of the stairs, listening.

He's a large, balding man, and he starts out by asking Mom and Dad if there can be no compromise between them in the sight of the Lord. "Remember, in First Corinthians we read, 'And unto the married I command, let not the wife depart from her husband.'" He looks at Mom to see if she has got that straight.

She won't look at him. He turns to Dad, who's sitting on the piano bench as far from Mom as he can get and still be in the same room. "And in the verse that follows, 'Let not the husband put away his wife.'" His earnest, jowly, troubled face looks up at Dad. He's holding the Bible, and he's clearly prepared to pour forth a lot more of it on them.

We don't dare speak, but I'm desperately fighting the urge to stand up and shout, "Yeah, hear that? You can't not be married!"

It's like Pastor Linkous is reading my mind and is speaking for me. He thumbs through the Bible rapidly. "Of course here in Mark we have the ultimate Word,

'What therefore God hath joined together, let not man put asunder.'" He brings his head down to look over the top of his glasses like he's checking, with each passage, to see if they get it. Mom and Dad are looking at him stonily.

He starts on a long prayer, and Mike and Johnny and I creep dejectedly back to our bedrooms.

The next day I say to Mom while we're at her stand, "I heard Pastor Linkous last night."

"Yeah," she sighs, "I guess he feels like he has to try, but there's really not much use."

The next night Deacon Lefever comes. He's a man I've only ever seen once or twice, but he's the sort of man I'd remember. He's tall, thin, and hawkish. But the thing that really stands out about him is the look in his eyes. They're black, and you feel like they'll burn if he looks at you. There's a kind of almost fire in them. When he talks, his voice is deep and powerful.

By the time the boys and I get to the top of the stairs to watch and listen, he has Mom and Dad sitting on the same sofa, side by side. He says they have to sit together, because he can't talk to them if they're apart. I'm thinking, way to go, Deac!

Then he begins a prayer, and his voice goes from being very loud to so soft it's almost a whisper, yet we have no trouble hearing him. His voice climbs to loud again, slowly, like he's using it to build something. It goes from low to loud, step by step, until the furniture is practically shaking.

Normally a prayer makes me sleepy, but his doesn't.

He talks to God about two people who are wandering in a wilderness with wild animals snarling and snapping at them. He makes the wilderness seem so dangerous and frightening that I feel like I have to look over my shoulder. He describes the hot breath of the animals that are coming to get them, and he prays for them to be delivered from the wild beasts of prey.

He calls Mom "Sister Gwen," and Dad "Brother Tim," and his voice rises to almost a shout when he tells about the dangers they're in. Then it falls to a hoarse whisper when he describes the path they must get on to save themselves and their marriage and their family.

Mike and Johnny and I look around at each other. I'm wondering if we're in the same jungle with Mom and Dad, just as lost, or if we're on the path they're trying to find. Like, maybe we're calling them to come up on the path with us, but they can't hear us.

He's almost got them out of the wilderness, and he ends the prayer with a thundering, "Amen."

I think he's finished, but he goes right into, "For in that great passage from Ephesians we read, 'Submit yourselves one to another in the fear of God.'"

His eyes bore into them. We can't see their faces, but it's obvious that he has all their attention. They're practically grasping each other for protection from him.

Suddenly, with no introduction, he leans forward. "Husbands, love your wives! Wives, submit yourselves unto your own husbands, as unto the Lord." The Holy Bible commands it!" The word "commands" is so loud, it bursts into the air. "'. . . men ought to love their wives as their own bodies'! This is a great mystery!" "Mystery" is shouted with a burst, too.

Then, in a quiet voice, and slapping his Bible shut to show that he is finished, he says, "'Let every one of you in particular so love his wife even as himself; and the wife see that she reverence her husband.'"

Mike and Johnny and I exchange wide-eyed glances. Mom and Dad are getting up, and we know they'll be turning around where they can see us, so we start to get up to hustle back down the hall. I'm the last one up, and I'm just turning carefully around when Deacon Lefever glances up and looks me straight in the eye. I quickly dash on tiptoe back down the hall. Of course the floor squeaks.

The next day Mom seems particularly thoughtful, but it's obvious that they're still in their separate parts of the house.

I tell my counselor that night, "My Mom and Dad need to come here more than I do."

21

Actually things are beginning to change. It seems like they are trying. Now we all join hands and pray every evening before we go to bed. Each of us has to say a prayer out loud.

During one of the prayers Mom tells God that she isn't going to mention the guns again.

Dad tells God he loves the guns, but he thinks Uncle Canute really enjoys having them at his place, so he and the boys can just go there when they want to work on them or shoot them.

At church on Sunday Pastor Linkous beams happily at all of us and says, "It's a fine thing to give 'to the greater glory of God.'"

I think things are going better because of Deacon Lefever, and when I see him after a couple of weeks I give him a big smile. Not that he even recognizes me.

Whenever I think about Bentley and mention her to anyone, Mom and Dad get us all together to pray, so I don't mention her much. When we do pray about her it's weird, because I say to God, "Please forgive Mike and Johnny for killing Bentley."

But Mike and Johnny say, "Please let Halley know that we didn't kill Bentley," and then Dad or Mom pray,

"Please ease our hearts about the loss of our beloved Bentley." So it's really something that only God can solve.

On Christmas morning, my present to Mom is a silver jelly spoon that I bought at an auction myself. I asked another lady to bid on it for me, and she did. The money came from pot holders I made from old nylons. They were an ugly brown, so I used a big needle and wove bright colored yarn all around the edges. Mom says she can sell every one of them I make.

My presents to Dad, Mike, and Johnny are gloves.

When all the presents are exchanged, there's still none from Mike and Johnny to me. I always keep close track of who I get presents from.

After everything else is opened, they get up and go out to the garage. Then, banging into everything and telling each other to be careful and to "watch out," they both come in carrying something huge and bulging. It's lumpy and it's covered with brown butcher paper. "This is for Halley," Johnny says. They both look proud to the max.

I jump up and run over to it, ready to grab it, but Mike puts his elbow up so I can't get to it. "You have to just tear the paper off while we hold it. It's explosive. If you aren't careful, it'll blow up the whole house."

Dad says, "What the . . . !"

Mom says, "Oh, it's explosive, all right. Stand back when she opens it, and wait for the explosion."

It's lumpy and very big. I dig loose an end of the butcher paper and begin tearing. There are blobs and blobs of crumpled-up newspaper glued to the butcher paper on the inside just to make it look lumpy. Under the blobs of newspaper is Christmas wrapping paper. My finger goes through the Christmas paper and strikes glass. Then I rip and tear and sweep the paper aside. It's my picture! I don't even look at it. I just run up to my room, crying.

Even hours later when we're eating, I'm quiet and I can hardly keep from crying. I've muttered a few dozen thank-you's, but nothing can make a thank-you the size that I feel.

We're having ham with raisin sauce, and I'm thinking, I guess this means I have to be nice to them forever. I really don't want to think about that.

Dad's saying, "You spent three hundred dollars! Where did you get it?" Mike scowls and looks out the window.

Johnny says, "Mom-Boots, and" —he swallows— "Henry."

"Henrico," I say with a grin.

Mike looks at me and laughs.

"But it was yours," Dad says. "You didn't need to do that. It was too much money. Old Edgar just asked that much to be greedy."

Mike says, "Yeah, well."

"Halley didn't get to stay in a beautiful estate for three weeks," Johnny says, "or jump on a huge, three-level trampoline."

"She had to stay here and go to school," Mike says. "And she missed swimming in the Olympic-size pool for hours every day and even at night."

"And throwing balls for the rottweilers. That was the most fun," Johnny says.

"And riding in the Maserati," Mike adds. They just go on and on about how great everything was and how I missed all of it. I have to hear tons of stuff, like how they had four trips to Busch Gardens and a ride around Manhattan Island on a boat.

Later in the afternoon I call Kirk to come up and see what I got. His loot is a hockey stick, good in-line hockey skates, and a bankbook. He shows me the balance: two hundred dollars.

"Did you know about them getting my picture?" I ask.

He's grinning and he nods. "Edgar told me."

"When?" I don't believe he can keep secrets from me.

"A couple of weeks ago."

I look at him like, "Yeah, right," but he goes on. "Edgar didn't tell me at first. He asked me what I'd get for Christmas if I had three hundred dollars to spend. I told him I didn't know, but then I guessed if I had three hundred dollars, I'd get you the picture so you'd have it. But he said it was already sold. Then he told me it was Mike and Johnny who bought it, and he was giving me the three hundred dollars he got for it. So I got skates and the stick with one of the hundreds, but I don't really want anything else, so I'm just saving the money for when I get old. If you'd really like to, you could use it to get another cat."

Actually, I think he's crazy. Christmas makes people nuts. He was going to buy me the picture! He and Edgar don't have a lot of money, or if they do they sure don't spend it on anything. They don't even live in a house. And yet he's going to use two hundred dollars to get me a cat?

His bike's old! They don't have nice furniture, just everything old. Edgar could probably use the money to buy some kind of fancy fake arms and legs that would work with computer chips so he could really stand.

I'm just staring at Kirk, so he gets up and leaves. He goes out to the driveway and starts playing roller basketball with Mike and Johnny. Mike says that some day basketball played on inline skates is going to be an Olympic sport and have big teams like other sports. Dad says he's nuts.

Mom and Dad get all emotional when they hear about Kirk and the money, and they both go and stand beside each other looking at my picture. "I'll have to get sinkers tomorrow so I can hang it," Dad murmurs. "Maybe she wouldn't mind if we hung it over the sofa. It's really too big for her room, and I kind of like it."

Mom says, "There's something about it. It's different . . . ! It's not . . . it has . . ."

Dad finishes for her, "Character," and she doesn't even resent it. A little voice inside of me says, "They're getting close again."

Later in the day, when it's suppertime, Mom suddenly exclaims, "Tim, we're going to take a Christmas dinner down to Kirk and Edgar. We'll take them some of everything. Do you know the two of them spent Christmas alone there?"

22

It's not really too cold, even though it's Christmas, so instead of driving we all get flashlights and troop down along the creek in the dark to the Dragon. We're each carrying something for Edgar and Kirk to eat.

When we knock on the door we hear Edgar's gruff voice demanding, "Who's that?" Kirk looks out the cob-webbed window and then opens the door. When he sees us all there with the bowls and things he looks too surprised to speak.

Mom gives a cheery, "Merry Christmas!" And before Edgar can get out anything, she steps in. Then Mike and Johnny and I and Dad pile in behind her.

Edgar looks dazed, and in his bulging eyes there's an even more unfriendly look than usual. I can see what they were doing before we came, playing chess.

Mom pulls up a wooden box to sit on, and she tells Mike and Johnny cheerily, "Sit down, boys."

To Edgar she says brightly, "Christmas dinner. I don't want any leftovers." She's smiling and she begins chat-ting so happily and persistently that the whole room seems to be getting warmer and brighter.

We're all sitting in a room that's so small we're practi-cally on top of each other. It's plain that she intends to stay. To Kirk she says, "I hope you're hungry. The gravy was so good this time. I usually burn the stock, or it gets lumpy or too salty or too peppery, but this time it came out perfect."

Kirk holds a plate out to Edgar, and the clamped hooks clank onto the edge. Then Kirk starts piling his plate hugely full. Edgar watches him for a moment, then mutters, "Thanks."

"Halley loves her picture," Dad says. "The boys really surprised us! They tell me the picture was from your home." It's really a question, and Dad leaves a large space for an answer, but Edgar's eating.

I've never seen him eat. His hooks hold the plate and manipulate the fork, rapidly, expertly. I think that Dad or Mom will just go on, because he's eating, but they don't. They just let the silence grow, looking at him expectantly.

Kirk begins to fidget. He reaches into a drawer under the table where the chess set is laid out and pulls out a deck of cards, then slides them back. There's a long, long silence, but finally, after chewing and swallowing for a long time, Edgar says, "Yes, the picture was in . . . our home."

Dad says carefully, "Kirk told Halley he wanted to use the rest of his money to buy her a cat. But Halley can get any old cat if she wants one. When she was four, she was very ill, so we just got Bentley then to humor her."

"Kirk really should keep his money," Mom says. "He told Halley he doesn't need it because his life here with you is perfect, but he should keep it."

Edgar's just looking at us. Held clamped in his right-hand hook is an embroidered, needleworked napkin that Mom tucked in the box with his meal, and he wipes his mouth carefully with it. I notice the remains of what must have been their Christmas dinner: a half-used family-size can of chicken noodle soup, a plastic bowl with a few pretzels still left in it, and two plastic cups with an opened can of Hawaiian punch.

Edgar's bulging eyes settle on Mom. "He said his life here with me is perfect?" His voice is more gruff than ever.

Mom's smiling and nodding with such warmth that I think she'll melt the furniture.

Edgar flips his hooked stick and shoves the plate back from the edge of the table. His eyes are on Kirk. "You're happy?"

Kirk nods and smiles.

"Well, well." He looks at Mom. "I wanted him to be, of course." Then he looks at me, and I have to control a sudden wild impulse to burst out of the room.

He goes on. "If he's happy, it's because of this little missy—" He means me. "She won't let him sit and mope. Ever since we came she has drawn him out, kept him moving, kept him on his toes."

He holds the cane over his eyes, and I think with absolute wonder that I'm seeing tears, but they quickly vanish and he goes on. "He was no good when we came here. He'd seen too much, been through too much."

I look at Kirk, but Kirk's looking at the floor.

Mom asks, gently, "Who are you, Edgar? Trust us with that. Let us know."

Edgar takes a deep breath. He's looking at the wooden

rafters that hold up the corrugated tin roof. With his hook he grasps the shiny, hot handle of the potbellied stove and swings open the door to reveal a mound of red coals. Using the left hooks with the right, he expertly maneuvers three split pieces of wood in upon the coals and slams the door shut again.

At first when Edgar starts to do something I think I want to do it for him, but then he does it so well I know I would just be in the way.

"My father was a Seneca, and my mother was a little red-haired Jewish woman. He was an abusive man, and he kicked her in the belly when she was pregnant with me.

"Her water broke, and she thought I was dead. When my father realized what he had done, he cried and beat his breast. My mother just despised and pitied him.

"She thought I would come immediately, and she thought I would be dead. But there was no birth. She had no labor. The doctors in the town and the tribal midwife told her that I was dead inside of her. That her body was a tomb, that eventually I would rot inside of her and kill her. She said, 'So be it,' and let it be.

"After weeks I was born in an agonizing, dry birth that she assumed was bringing forth a dead thing, but when she saw me and that I was alive, she thought I was beautiful. She had expected something dead and rotten, you see. But she told me that instead, she looked into beautiful, expressive eyes. This is what she said" — it's like Edgar is going away, and he's reciting some ancient poem from a faraway place— "and a beautiful nose, and a beautiful body, with tiny, beautiful little hands and ears and mouth. She used the word 'beautiful' to describe my features so much, I began to count them. I asked her over and over, and if she missed one I reminded her.

"True, I am deformed, but she rejoiced in what I was, because I was not the loathsome, rotten thing she expected. The sheer fact that I was alive was beautiful to her.

"No one could understand her joy. They thought she was insane, that her suffering and fear had made her insane. The universal opinion was that I should have died, and she, somehow, being Jewish and therefore a sorceress, had cheated the Great Spirit, although not entirely.

"My life was viewed as the result of witchcraft on her part and evil brutality on the part of my father. No one wanted anything to do with us. We were banished to a lonesome part of the reservation, like unclean things.

"When I was four, she left my father to his fate and took me and went to live with her family in Brooklyn. But to them when they saw me I was just as loathsome. They thought she was insane to have ever married him—she admitted to me, once, that she only married him out of some misplaced sense of idealism, a concept of Indians as noble, and all that.

"In New York we went from being isolated to being surrounded by throngs of people. From no eyes to thousands of eyes, all of them looking at me, or so I thought. And I became a terror, I can tell you. They didn't need to scorn or pity me. But at night, when it was just the two of us, alone, over and over I asked her to tell me the story of how she had lost the water I floated in, and everyone thought I was rotten and hideous, but how beautiful I was to her.

"One night when I was seven she began to tell the story, but when she got to the 'beautiful' part she skipped it. She did the lost water part, and the part where I was born and she saw I wasn't rotten, but instead of saying how beautiful she thought I was, she said, 'And instead of a rotten thing, what do I have?' There was such delight in her eyes, but I was afraid, because if the story changed maybe she was finally seeing me as hideously deformed like everyone else.

"But when I protested because it was different, she said, 'I have such a clever, capable child. With so little—no arms, no legs, no feet—you dress yourself, feed yourself, go to the bathroom, get up, get down, go here, go there. Whatever it is that needs to be done, you find a way. You always were beautiful, but that's nothing. It's of no consequence, and beauty always fades. But to be clever and capable, and that's what you are, that's a thing that lasts.

"I wasn't sure, but I let her go on. She said, 'I was worried, I'll admit it. I thought, beautiful as he is, what if he can't manage? But manage you do. Being capable and clever are rare gifts.'

"After that night I never asked her again to tell me about myself. I tucked the image of myself as 'clever and capable' in my heart.

"She died when I was twelve, and then I was on my

own in an unforgiving city with people who didn't care about me." He waves his sticks and glances at us, briefly, before his eyes go back to the highest beams.

The fire in the stove has begun crackling, and warmth is radiating throughout the room. Mom nods encouragingly, and Dad smiles contentedly. Kirk is making a house of cards.

"When I was older, another woman saw me, and we discovered that we could laugh together. Her name was Wilhelmina, and we were married. She had cerebral palsy. But, you know, we loved to dance. Now you might think that was ridiculous, but we did. We went to dances three nights a week, and people got in a circle around us and clapped when we took the floor. We had much laughter, and we had a daughter. My wife, Wilhelmina, didn't live long. Too soon it was up to me to care for our girl."

Kirk has stopped the card house and he's looking at Edgar curiously, waiting for the next words. I suddenly know that he has never heard this part before.

"She was such a perfect child, Angela, to have come from us. She was bright and normal, beautiful and good. When she grew up she married a good choice, Kenneth Demitros. He was half Irish and half Greek, a fine young man. But they went to live in Ireland with his mother, and that was their end.

"I thought for a long time their wrong choice came from my curse, that maybe they were right in calling me a mistake.

"I was there in Ireland visiting my girl. She wanted me to come and live with them.

"They had five children, Kirk the youngest. We were in town to get the middle boy's glasses fixed, and I was sitting outside of the shop with Kirk when the whole street exploded.

"Kirk was just four years old, standing by me. We were thrown across the street. In an instant my daughter was gone, and her husband, and her children. Of eight only two remained. Only Kirk and I. In an instant he was all that was left, and me."

Mom and Dad and Mike and Johnny all look like they wish they'd gone home a while before, back when Edgar was telling about being beautiful, or even when he was telling about dancing. Kirk's just looking at him with his mouth open, and I know he has never heard about his family or his mother before.

Edgar's leaning back in his soft, leather chair. I can see it's a match for the leather sofa and two other club chairs that were near my picture. I can see, also, that there wouldn't be room in the small place where they live for the rest of the furniture.

Edgar's two sticks are crossed in front of him, the hooks resting on his foot-booties. He says, with his eyes shut, "I thought my mother's vision was, perhaps, wrong, and my father's people were right that I was cursed. But if it's true, and it may be, I'm content now to play what life deals. So, Kirk's happy with me! Well, well, well."

I'm really afraid to ask, but I want to know. "Why did you shoot your donkey?"

Kirk looks at me, shocked, but Edgar doesn't seem to

mind the question. "Bitterness. It was bitterness. I brought Kirk back to the reservation where I was born. I thought green fields and flowers and bees would be best. But the old troubles were there, so we came here and I changed my name to his.

"It's what I have lived, always. Disputes and more disputes, with no peace. Always the same. They even found me here. I thought I could get away, but men are always coming, wanting me to testify. I'm tired of talking. I don't want to testify. If I wanted to talk of brutal things, I could talk to you . . . about the cat."

Suddenly all of our eyes are upon him. From the Seneca reservation to New York City to Ireland, it's all his life. But now it's like he's crossing a bridge to our lives.

My eyes go to Kirk, questioningly. He lifts his eyebrow and shrugs.

Edgar closes his eyes. "I saw those neighbors of yours one evening. They were shooting at something white, a pet rabbit, I thought. Even after they shot it and picked it up by one back leg, I couldn't tell.

"Kirk tells me there has been a suspicion in your family that these boys" —he indicates Mike and Johnny— "killed the girl's cat. It's no concern of mine, but I'm certain that the cat was not killed by anyone in this room."

Kirk turns his gaze to me and shakes his head slowly.

"The Sowers shot Bentley?" Dad asks. We're all looking at each other. Then he exclaims, "The stinking trash! They stand in their backyard and swear at us, but I never dreamed . . . I didn't realize!"

164

Mom is shaking her head. "But, why! How could people do such a thing! Why did I never think it was them!"

Dad leans toward Edgar and speaks earnestly. "So you think they . . . Edgar, thank you! This thing has been a wound in our family that would never quite heal . . . ! Thank you for telling us!"

I get up and race out the door. Somehow it's worse now that I know how it really was. Always before it was never real to me. I never could see it. Mike and Johnny did it, I thought. But now I know she was with cruel, vicious people at the end, frightened and alone.

I go down to the edge of the pond and sit crying in the dark and cold. Kirk comes out to sit beside me. "Why didn't Edgar tell us about this before?"

Kirk thinks awhile before he answers. "Probably because he believes in minding his own business. If he had told me before, I would have told you."

I glance at him. "Yeah, I know. It would've made things simpler."

Kirk says, "I don't think he trusted anybody for a long time, but now I think he might trust some people."

I'm looking out across the cold pond. "I can't believe they picked Bentley up by one leg and held her with her blood dripping out!"

He has a stick and he's rubbing the end of it on the stone abutment. At first it's like he's doing it for no reason, but then I see he's slowly sharpening it to a point.

"Eddie and Gary!" I exclaim with a wail. "They probably were the ones who actually shot her! I bet they've been laughing about it all this time."

Kirk is holding the stick like it's a lance. He begins sorting it out. "They probably brought her back to their house, dead. And then they threw her in your garden. It wouldn't have been hard to catch her. She was so gentle. They could've picked her up easily." I glance at him. He's jabbing the stick into the air, again and again.

I begin to cry a lot more. "And all this time I thought it was Mike and Johnny."

"I didn't," Kirk says. "Gary told a kid that his mom screams all the time about your family."

"Why! They're so evil!"

"Yeah."

The next day Mom calls the police to complain about the Sowers killing Bentley. A police car pulls into the Sowers' driveway, but after they finish talking to them, they come over to our house to report, and it's just, "The Sowers deny it, and Edgar Demitros can't testify for sure that it was a cat they were shooting. We don't have enough proof to charge them."

Mike comes home the next day and tells us that his friend heard Eddie Sower brag about killing Bentley and getting away with it. In our family prayer circle I say, "I want the Sowers punished, God."

When we get around to Dad, he says, "I'm sure You'll do the right thing when it comes to the Sowers, God. We're content to leave it in Your hands."

I'm making a lot of pot holders and saving all the money for new school jackets for Mike and Johnny. They both want them, but Mom says they're too expensive. They'll really be surprised when one day they just find the jackets hanging in their closets.

My counselor has stopped talking about me and started asking me what he should do about his children. Dad says I can start charging him for advice.

Uncle Canute has the guns. Dad says, "Canute spends hours petting and restoring those guns. When he gets done, they'll be too valuable to shoot."

In our family prayer circle Mom says, "Now Halley wants to learn to shoot, God. Can You see how much I need Your help?" She says it with a grin.

EPILOGUE

David is selling the lease to his stand, packing up, and leaving. Dad is helping him pack. They knew each other a long time ago.

The lady who's going to take it over shows Dad a puppy she got at the pound. "Weren't you the people who owned that beautiful Persian cat?" she asks. Dad tells her what happened, and she says, "I don't know if you'd be interested, but there's a litter of long-haired, whitish kittens at the pound." He doesn't say anything. He waits for me to ask. Of course I do.

Mike and Johnny have to go along with us when we go. They have to have an opinion on everything.

There are only three kittens left, and they're Himalayans, not Persians, but they're as fluffy as Bentley. The woman who manages the animal shelter says everyone wants one until she tells them how much grooming they need. She tells everyone you have to spend most of your life combing them or they'll die of a hair ball, so no one takes them. She only wants people to take them who pledge they are willing to spend every minute of the rest of their lives grooming them.

Mom tells her we had a Persian and we know what's involved. Then she says the kitten is for me, and the

woman starts a whole new line about how a child can
never take on such an awesome responsibility.

Mom's getting hot, and she says that I groomed
Bentley all the time since I was four, and Bentley would
have lived to be twenty-six if a vicious neighbor hadn't
shot her. Then the lady says, "Oh, you have vicious
neighbors. Well, we wouldn't want to put any of them
where they're going to get shot."

While Mom's talking, Mike and Johnny are forming
the plan that since there are three kittens and three of
us, we should have them all.

My attention is drawn two cages away to a giant,
wise-eyed, tortoiseshell cat that's sitting, watching me.
Not them. Not anybody else, just me. He introduces
himself with his stare. "My name is Ebenezer," his stare
says. Something like Scrooge. I say softly as I kneel by
his cage, "Ebenezer, Ebenezer, Ebenezer."

Mrs. Oh-so-cautious, the Pound Lady, calls to me,
"Stay away from him, dear, he bites."

I turn around to look at her and then back to him, and
I have to force myself not to laugh. He bites! Ha, ha,
ha. He's huge and beautiful, and he raises his head so he
can continue to look at me. Of course he bites. That's
perfect! That's splendid! The Sowers won't get him. If
they try to get him, he'll bite them. But he won't bite
me. I'll cover my hand with baby food chicken and
then just sit in the room with him when he's hungry.

He can come over to me, or he can wait awhile.
When he does come, he can lick the chicken off my
hand or bite it. Which does she think he'll do?

I start my campaign for him immediately, but the woman is determined that he can't be a family cat. Certainly not a cat designated for a child. She'll not even release him to a family that has a child.

Mike asks the pointed question, "How long has he been here?" Pointed questions are Mike's specialty.

"Ten days," the lady says. Her tone is clipped.

"How long do you keep them before . . ." Mom asks.

"Not much longer than ten days, in fact . . ."

"Mom," I scream, "they're going to kill him!"

To the lady, Mom says, "We'll take him."

The lady starts again about him biting and not being a family cat, but Mom interrupts, "He's for my aged mother, who lives in an apartment alone. She desperately needs a companion, and since I'm with her a good part of each day, I'll be able to take care of him for her."

Curtains come down over our eyes, but behind them we're terribly shocked. Mom's mother has been dead for twenty years. She's telling a flat-out lie.

Ebenezer comes home in a carrier and goes immediately into Bentley's crate.

I lie in front of the crate for the rest of the day and tell him how important he is to me.

Mom comes over and stoops down to look at him. "Those eyes!" she exclaims. "He looks like he possesses endless wisdom."

"That's what I'll call him, 'Wisdom,'" I tell her. "He was Ebenezer, but he's going to be Wisdom."

Mike's at the table eating a sandwich. "Yeah, call him 'Wizz.' That fits him." Johnny's laughing so hard he's falling off the chair. "Or, 'Dumb.' 'Wizz Dumb.' Old Wizzdumb. Yeah, that fits."

"Mom, make them stop!"

Mom says, "I could sooner turn the tide. Wisdom's a fine name for him, and if people" —she gives them a look— "want to mock it, let them. My mother is with me in spirit always, so I wasn't too far from the truth, and she used to say, 'Mockery is the sport of small minds.'"

Later that afternoon Kirk comes. His eyes are shining with pure delight, and he has something cupped in his hands. From the way he looks I expect he's gone out and stubbed his toe on a zillion-dollar emerald.

For a short while he makes us guess while he holds the mystery, but then the mystery meows, and he opens his hands to reveal the tiniest, most fragile of the Himalayan kittens from the pound. "Edgar took me to get it," he says with wonder. "It was the last one."

I'm amazed, but Mike asks, indignantly, "How come they gave it to you? They wouldn't give it to us."

Kirk answers, "When Edgar said he wanted it, the lady looked at him like he was being ridiculous, and she started telling him he couldn't take care of it with his 'disability.' But he roared at her so loud she backed up, and fell over the waste can and landed on her butt. The whole time while she was getting up she just kept looking at his hooks." Kirk's eyes are dancing in a way I've never seen them before, and I feel like constantly jumping up and down.

"So, then what?"

"She just went and got it and handed it to me. She never even told him one other thing."

I reach for the kitten, and he lets me take it and cup it in my hands. "She's so small and soft!" I exclaim. "What's her name?"

He's looking at her with a pride and tenderness I've never seen. "When I got her I was thinking of Bentley, so I named her 'Rolls-Royce.'"

Mike and Johnny start laughing, and they keep it up until they drop off their stools and are rolling around on the floor, but Kirk doesn't even look embarrassed or act like he notices them. He just goes on, "Because, you know, Bentleys and Rolls-Royces are almost the same, except for their grilles, and she's a lot like Bentley, except for her nose."